CELTIC
TALES

CELTIC TALES

Fairy Tales and Stories of Enchantment

FROM

Ireland, Scotland, Brittany, and Wales

ILLUSTRATIONS BY

Kate Forrester

CHRONICLE BOOKS

SAN FRANCISCO

Library of Congress Cataloging-in-Publication Data
Title: Celtic tales : fairy tales and stories of enchantment from Ireland,
    Scotland, Brittany, and Wales.
Description: San Francisco : Chronicle Books, 2016.
Identifiers: LCCN 2015033485 | ISBN 978-1-4521-5175-5 (alk. paper)
Subjects: LCSH: Celts—Folklore. | Tales—Ireland. | Tales—Scotland. |
    Tales—France—Brittany. | Tales—Wales.
Classification: LCC GR137.C48 2016 | DDC 398.209417—dc23 LC record available at
http://lccn.loc.gov/2015033485

Manufactured in China.

Designed by Emily Dubin
Illustrations by Kate Forrester
Text adaptation by Mirabelle Korn

10 9

Chronicle Books LLC
680 Second Street
San Francisco, CA 94107
www.chroniclebooks.com

Chronicle books and gifts are available at special quantity discounts to corporations, professional associations, literacy programs, and other organizations.
For details and discount information, please contact our premiums department at corporatesales@chroniclebooks.com or at 1-800-759-0190.

———

"Do not think the fairies are always little.
Everything is capricious about them, even their size. . . .
Their chief occupations are feasting, fighting, and making
love, and playing the most beautiful music."

—WILLIAM BUTLER YEATS,
Fairy and Folk Tales of the Irish Peasantry

———

CONTENTS

———

1

—

TRICKSTERS

THE CLUMSY BEAUTY
and HER AUNTS

Ireland

here was once a poor widow with a daughter named Ursula, who was as beautiful as a spring day but as clumsy as could be. The poor mother was the most industrious person in the town, and was a particularly good hand at the spinning wheel. It was her greatest wish that her daughter should be as handy as herself so that she would find a good husband, but any work Ursula touched seemed to tangle or break in her fingers at once.

One morning, things were very bad, for Ursula had tried her hand at spinning once again, and once again had tangled the thread. Her mother was giving her a good scolding, when who should be riding by their small farm but the king's own son.

"Oh dear, oh dear, good woman," he said, "you must have a very bad child to make you scold so terribly. Sure it can't be this handsome girl who's vexed you!"

Now the widow knew the prince was in need of a wife, and she quickly devised a plan. "Oh, please, Your Majesty, not at all," she said. "I was only checking her for working herself too much. Would Your Majesty believe it? She spins three pounds of flax in a day, weaves it into linen the next, and makes it all into shirts the day after."

"Gracious," said the prince, "then she's the very lady that will catch my mother's eye, for she herself is the greatest spinner in the kingdom. Will you fetch your daughter's bonnet and cloak please, madam, and set her behind me on my horse? Why, my mother will be so delighted with her that perhaps she'll allow us to marry within the week. That is, of course, if the young lady herself is agreeable."

Well, the woman bundled Ursula into her bonnet and cloak and sent her off with the prince before the girl could even protest. But as they rode back to the castle together, the prince was so solicitous and kind that she almost forgot her fear of being found out.

When they arrived at the castle, the queen came out to meet her son and was almost struck dumb when she saw a young country girl sitting behind him. But when they dismounted and she saw the girl's handsome face and heard about her incredible feats of spinning, her feelings changed quite quickly. Ursula trembled under the queen's gaze, but the prince whispered in her ear that, if she didn't object to becoming his wife, she should strive to please his mother, so she smiled bravely and made a wobbly curtsy.

That evening they all dined together, and the prince and Ursula were getting fonder and fonder of one another, but the thought of spinning still sent a chill to her heart. And sure enough, after they had feasted, the queen led Ursula to a beautiful bedroom, pointed to a heap of fine flax in the corner, and said, "You may begin as soon as you like tomorrow morning, and I'll expect to see these three pounds in nice thread the morning after." Then she bid Ursula goodnight.

The poor girl slept little that night. And when she was left alone the next morning, she began her spinning with a heavy heart. Though she had a nice mahogany wheel and the finest flax she'd ever seen, the thread seemed to break every time she touched it. One moment it was as fine as a cobweb and the next as coarse as wool. At last, she pushed her chair back, let her hands fall into her lap, and burst out crying.

Just then, a small old woman with surprisingly big feet appeared before her, as if out of nowhere, and said, "What ails you, you handsome girl?"

"Oh," cried Ursula, "haven't I all that flax to spin before tomorrow morning, and I'll never be able to have even five yards of fine thread of it put together."

"And would you think it bad to ask poor Colliach Cushmōr to your wedding with the young prince? If you promise to invite me, all three pounds of your flax will be made into the finest of thread while you're taking your sleep tonight."

Ursula was overjoyed. "Indeed, you must be there and welcome, and I'll honor you all the days of your life."

"Very well," said Colliach Cushmōr. "Stay in your room 'til teatime and then tell the queen she may come in for her thread as early as she likes tomorrow morning."

Ursula did as she said, and the old woman was as good as her promise. The next morning, Ursula woke to find thread finer and evener than the gut of fly-fishers.

"What a brave girl," cried the queen. "I'll get my own mahogany loom brought to you, but you needn't do anything more today. Work and rest, work and rest, that's my motto. Tomorrow you'll weave all this thread, and who knows what may happen?" she added with a smile.

So Ursula spent another day with the prince, and she was so happy in his company that she almost forgot the task ahead of her. But the next morning when she sat down at the queen's loom, she was even more frightened than before. Her trembling fingers couldn't even put the warp in the gears, nor use the shuttle. She was sitting there in the greatest grief when a little old woman with mightily wide hips suddenly appeared before her. She said her name was Colliach Cromanmōr, and she offered the same bargain as Colliach Cushmōr. Eagerly, Ursula accepted, and great was the queen's pleasure the next morning when Ursula showed her linen as fine and white as the finest paper.

"What a darling girl," said the queen. "Take your ease with the ladies and gentlemen today, and if you have all this made into nice shirts tomorrow, you may present one of them to my son and be married to him out of my hand."

Oh, how poor Ursula trembled the next day as she sat with scissors, needle, and thread in hand. She was so near the prince now, and yet maybe would be soon so far from him. But she waited patiently 'til, a minute after noon, an old woman with a big red nose appeared before her. The woman introduced herself as Colliach Shron Mor Rua, and she made the same offer as the two before her. Ursula accepted with relief, and sure enough, when the queen paid her an early visit the next morning, there were a dozen fine shirts lying on the table.

THE WEDDING TOOK PLACE A FEW DAYS LATER, and it was exceedingly grand. Ursula's mother was there along with the rest, and at the wedding dinner, the queen could talk of nothing but the lovely shirts, and how happy she and the bride would be after the honeymoon, when they would be spinning and weaving and sewing shirts without end. The bridegroom didn't much like the conversation, and the bride liked it less, but before either could interject, a footman came up to the head of the table and said to the bride, "Your ladyship's aunt, Colliach Cushmōr, bade me ask if she might come in."

The bride blushed and wished she were seven miles under the floor, but she nodded. And the prince said, "Tell Mrs. Cushmōr that any relation of my bride's will always be heartily welcome wherever she and I are."

In came the woman with the big foot, and she got a seat near the queen. But the queen, who didn't like the interruption, soon asked rather spitefully, "Dear madam, what's the reason your foot is so big?"

"Faith, Your Majesty," said Colliach Cushmōr, "I was standing almost all my life at the spinning wheel, and that's the reason."

"I declare to you, my darling," said the prince, horrified, "I'll never allow you to spend one hour at the same spinning wheel."

A little while later, the footman approached again and said, "Your ladyship's aunt, Colliach Cromanmōr, wishes to come in, if you have no objection."

The prince and Ursula said she was welcome, and she took her seat and drank healths aplenty to the company.

But after a minute the queen said, "May I ask, madam, why you're so wide halfway between the head and the feet?"

"That, Your Majesty, is owing to sitting all my life at the loom," said Colliach Cromanmōr.

"By my scepter," said the prince, "my wife shall never sit there an hour."

Finally the footman approached again and said, "Your ladyship's aunt, Colliach Shron Mor Rua, is asking leave to come into the banquet."

Again the bride and bridegroom said she was welcome, and in came the old woman and settled herself at the table.

"Madam," said the queen, "will you tell us, if you please, why your nose is so big and red?"

"Troth, Your Majesty, my head was bent down over the stitching all my life, and all the blood in my body ran into my nose," said Colliach Shron Mor Rua.

"My darling," said the prince in all seriousness to Ursula, "if I ever see a needle in your hand, I'll run a hundred miles from you."

And in this way, the clumsy Ursula was relieved of spinning work for the rest of her life, and she and the prince were happily married at last.

MASTER and MAN

Ireland

illy Mac Daniel was once as good-natured a young man as ever shook his brogue at a festival, emptied a quart, or handled a shillelagh. He feared for nothing but the want of drink, cared for nothing but who should pay for it, and thought of nothing but how to make fun over it. Drunk or sober, a word and a blow was ever the way with Billy Mac Daniel, and a mighty easy way it is of either getting into or of ending a dispute. More's the pity that, through his fearing and caring and thinking for nothing but drink, this same Billy Mac Daniel fell into bad company—for surely the fairies are the worst of all company anyone could come across.

It so happened that Billy was going home one clear frosty night not long after Christmas. The moon was round and bright, but although it was as fine a night as heart could wish for, he felt pinched with cold. "By my word," chattered Billy, "a drop of good liquor would be no bad thing to keep a man's soul from freezing in him, and I wish I had a full measure of the best."

"Never wish it twice, Billy," said a voice right beside him.

He looked down and saw a little man in a three-cornered hat, bound all about with gold lace, and with great silver buckles on his shoes, which were so big that it was a wonder he could wear them. He held out a glass as big as himself, filled with as good liquor as ever eye looked on or lip tasted.

"Success, my little fellow," said Billy Mac Daniel, nothing daunted, though well he knew that the little man belonged to the good people. "Here's to your health, and thank you kindly." And he took the glass and drained it to the very bottom without ever taking a second breath to it.

"Success," said the little man, "and you're heartily welcome, Billy. But don't think to cheat me as you have done others. Out with your purse and pay me like a gentleman."

"Is it I pay you?" said Billy. "Could I not just take you up and put you in my pocket as easily as a blackberry?"

"Billy Mac Daniel," said the little man, getting very angry, "you shall be my servant for seven years and a day, and that is the way I will be paid. So make ready to follow me."

When Billy heard this he began to be very sorry for having used such bold words towards the little man. Yet, without knowing why, he felt himself obliged to follow the little man about the country that whole night, up and down, over hedge and ditch, and through bog and break without any rest.

When morning began to dawn, the little man turned round to him and said, "You may now go home, Billy. But on your peril, don't fail to meet me in the Fort-Field tonight, or it may be the worse for you in the long run. If I find you a good servant, you will find me an indulgent master."

Home went Billy Mac Daniel, and though he was tired and weary enough, and stayed in bed all that day, he couldn't get a wink of sleep for thinking of the little man. He was afraid not to do his bidding, so up he got in the evening and away he went to the Fort-Field.

It was not long before the little man arrived and said, "Billy, I want to go on a long journey tonight. So saddle one of my horses, and you may saddle another for yourself, as you are to go along with me and may be tired after your walk last night."

Billy thought this very considerate of his master and thanked him accordingly. "But," said he, "if I may be so bold, sir, I would ask which is the way to your stable, for never a thing do I see but the old fort here and the old thorn tree in the corner of the field and the stream running at the bottom of the hill and the bit of bog beside it with the rushes growing in it."

"Ask no questions, Billy," said the little man, "but go over to that bit of bog and bring me two of the strongest rushes you can find."

Billy did accordingly, wondering what the little man would be at. He picked two of the stoutest rushes he could find, and brought them back to his master.

"Get up, Billy," said the little man, taking one of the rushes from him and striding across it.

"Where shall I get up, please your honor?" said Billy.

"Why, up on horseback, like me, to be sure," said the little man.

"Is it after making a fool of me you'd be," said Billy, "bidding me get on horseback upon that bit of a rush? Maybe you want to persuade me that the rush I pulled a minute ago out of the bog over there is in fact a horse?"

"Up! Up! And no words," said the little man, looking very angry. "The best horse you ever rode was but a fool next to these."

So Billy, thinking all this was a joke, but fearing to vex his master, straddled across the rush.

"Borram! Borram! Borram!" cried the little man suddenly.

Immediately, the rushes swelled up into fine horses, and away they went at full speed. But Billy, who had put the rush between his legs without much minding how he did it, found himself sitting on horseback the wrong way, which was rather awkward, with his face to the horse's tail. So quickly had his steed started off with him that he had no power to turn around, and there was therefore nothing for it but to hold on by the tail.

At last they came to their journey's end, and stopped at the gate of a fine house.

"Now, Billy," said the little man, "do as you see me do, and follow me close. But as you did not know your horse's head from its tail, mind that your own head does not spin round until you can't tell whether you are standing on it or on your heels. For remember that old liquor, though it can make a cat speak, can make a man dumb."

The little man then said some queer kind of words, out of which Billy could make no meaning. But he managed to say the words anyway, and as soon as he did, he felt himself flying alongside the little man—though he didn't know how—in through the keyhole of the door, and through one keyhole after another until they reached the wine cellar, which was well stored with all kinds of wine.

The little man fell to drinking as hard as he could, and Billy, in no way disliking the example, did the same. "The best of masters are you, surely," said Billy to him, "and I will be well pleased to be in your service if you continue to give me plenty to drink."

"I have made no bargain with you," said the little man, "and will make none. But get up and follow me now."

Away they went again, through keyhole after keyhole. Then each mounted upon the rush which he had left at the hall door, and they scampered off, kicking the clouds before them like snowballs as soon as the words "Borram, Borram, Borram" had passed their lips.

When they came back to the Fort-Field, the little man dismissed Billy, bidding him to be there the next night at the same hour. Thus did they go on, night after night, shaping their course one night here and another night there, sometimes north, sometimes east, sometimes south, and sometimes west, until there was not a gentleman's wine cellar in all Ireland they had not visited—and they could tell the flavor of every wine in every cellar as well as or better than the butler himself.

One night when Billy Mac Daniel met the little man as usual in the Fort-Field and was going to the bog to fetch the horses for their journey, his master said to him, "Billy, I shall want another horse tonight, for maybe we will bring back more company than we take."

So Billy, who now knew better than to question any order given to him by his master, brought a third rush, wondering who it might be that would travel back in their company, and whether he was about to have a fellow servant. "If it is another servant," thought Billy, "he shall go and fetch the horses from the bog every night, for I don't see why I am not, every inch of me, as good a gentleman as my master."

Well, away they went, with Billy leading the third horse, and never stopped until they came to a snug farmer's house in County Limerick. Within the house there was great carousing, and the little man stopped outside for some time to listen.

Then, turning round all of a sudden, he said, "Billy, I will be a thousand years old tomorrow!"

"God bless us, sir," said Billy in surprise. "Will you?"

"Don't say those words again, Billy," said the little old man, "or you will be my ruin forever. Now, as I will be a thousand years in the world tomorrow, I think it is full time for me to get married."

"I think so, too, without any kind of doubt at all," said Billy, "if ever you mean to marry."

"And to that purpose," said the little man, "have I come all the way to this house. For in this house, this very night, is young Darby Riley going to be married to Bridget Rooney. And as Bridget is a tall and comely girl and has come of decent people, I think of marrying her myself and taking her off with me."

"And what will Darby Riley say to that?" said Billy.

"Silence!" and the little man, putting on a mighty severe look. "I did not bring you here with me to ask questions."

Without holding further argument, he began saying the queer words which had the power of passing him through keyholes as free as air, and which Billy thought himself mighty clever to be able to say after him. Into the house they both went, and up to the rafters, for the better viewing of the company and to keep out of sight. The little man perched himself up as nimbly as a sparrow on one of the big beams which went across the house over the heads of the guests, and Billy did the same upon another facing him. But as he was not much accustomed to roosting in such a place, his legs hung down as untidy as may be, while the little man sat contentedly upon his haunches.

There they sat, both master and man, looking down upon the fun that was going forward. Under them were the priest and the piper; the father of Darby Riley and Darby's two brothers; the father and the mother of Bridget Rooney and her four sisters, with brand-new ribbons in their caps, and her three brothers all looking as clean and as clever as any three boys in Munster; and enough uncles and aunts and cousins besides to make a full house of it. And on the table there was plenty to eat and drink for every one of the guests, as if they had been double the number.

Now, just as Mrs. Rooney was helping the priest to the first cut of the pig's head, Billy saw his master take a little leather pouch from his pocket and, reaching into it, pull out a pinch of some powder that he sprinkled down upon the table right in front of the bride. At that, the bride gave a sneeze. It made everyone at the table start, but not a soul said "God bless us." All the guests thought that the priest would have done so, as was his duty, and no one wished to take the word out of his mouth, which, unfortunately, was preoccupied with pig's head and greens. But after a moment's pause the fun and merriment of the bridal feast went on without the pious benediction.

Both Billy and his master noticed this happen from their stations high up in the rafters.

"Ha!" exclaimed the little man, and his eye twinkled with a strange light. "Ha!" said he, leering down at the bride. "I have half of her now, surely. Let her sneeze but twice more and she is mine."

Again he sprinkled a bit of the mysterious powder down upon the table, and again the fair Bridget sneezed. But she did it so gently, blushing with embarrassment, that few, except the little man and Billy, seemed to take any notice, and no one thought of saying "God bless us."

Billy all this time was regarding the poor girl with a most rueful expression, for he could not help thinking what a terrible thing it was for a nice young girl of nineteen, with large blue eyes, transparent skin, and dimpled cheeks suffused with health and joy, to be obliged to marry an ugly little bit of a man, who was a thousand years old, barring a day.

At this critical moment the bride gave a third sneeze and Billy roared out with all his might, "God bless us!"

Whether this exclamation resulted from his thoughts about the marriage or from the mere force of habit, he never could tell exactly. But no sooner was it uttered than the little man, his face glowing with rage and disappointment, sprung up from the beam on which he had perched himself and shrieked out in a shrill voice like a cracked bagpipe, "I discharge you from my service, Billy Mac Daniel—take that for your wages."

And he gave poor Billy a most furious kick in the back, which sent his unfortunate servant sprawling upon his face right in the middle of the supper table.

If Billy was astonished, how much more so was every one of the company into which he was thrown with so little ceremony. But when he had told his story, the priest laid down his knife and fork and married the young couple with all speed. And Billy Mac Daniel danced and drank and feasted to his heart's content at their wedding.

THE KILDARE POOKA

Ireland

nce upon a time, there was a big manor house in County Kildare, whose owner was often out of the country on business. When he was away, the servants were left alone to keep up the house, and sometimes they would let things go a bit more than they would have if their master had been home. But, as if the kitchen were rebelling against being left in disarray, the servants would often hear at night a frightful banging of the kitchen door and clattering of fire irons, pots, plates, and dishes. The longer this went on, the more terrified they all became, and none of them dared to enter the kitchen after the fire had died down at night.

One evening they sat up ever so long by the fire, however, telling each other stories about ghosts and fairies. They talked so long that the little scullery boy fell asleep right there, curled in the hearth, and he did not wake when they all tramped off to bed.

Later, after they were all gone, he was woken by the noise of the kitchen door opening. Startled and suddenly afraid, he peeped out from the hearth, and what should he see but a big donkey, standing and yawning before the dormant fire. The boy was about to come out from his hiding place and lead the animal back to the barn, when he saw it look around, scratch its ears, and say, "I may as well begin first as last."

The poor boy's teeth began to chatter, for now he knew this was no ordinary donkey, but a pooka. "Now he's going to eat me, surely," he thought.

But the pooka had something else to do. He stirred the fire, and then he brought in a pail of water from the pump and filled a big pot which he put on the fire. After that, he lay down before the fire, so close by the scullery boy that he dared not breathe. At last, the pot boiled, and the pooka rose again and began a flurry of activity.

There wasn't a plate or a dish or a spoon in that kitchen that he didn't fetch and put into the pot. He washed and dried the whole set as well as any kitchen maid and put them all up on the shelves again. Then he gave the floor a good and thorough sweeping. The last thing he did was to rake up the fire, and finally he walked out, just as nonchalantly as he had come, giving the door a good slam as he went.

Well, there was a hullaballoo the next morning when the poor scullery boy told his story. The servants could talk of nothing else the whole day. One said one thing, another said another, but one lazy scullery girl said the wittiest thing of all. "Well!" says she. "If the pooka does be cleaning up everything that way when we are asleep, what should we be slaving ourselves for doing his work?"

So said, so done. Not a bit of a plate or dish saw a drop of water that evening, and not a broom was laid on the floor. Everyone went to bed soon after sundown. Next morning, everything was as fine as fine in the kitchen, and the lord mayor might have eaten his dinner off the flagstones. It was a great relief to the servants, and everything went well until the scullery boy, who was now proud of his adventure and had forgotten all his fear, declared that he would stay up one night and have a chat with the pooka.

He waited by the fire, in plain sight this time, and to tell the truth, he was a little daunted when the door was thrown open and the pooka appeared. But he plucked up his courage and said, "Good evening, sir."

"Good evening," said the pooka.

"If it isn't taking a liberty," said the boy, "might I ask who you are and why you are so kind as to do half of the day's work for us every night?"

"No liberty at all," said the pooka. "I'll tell you and willingly. I was a servant in the time of your master's father, and was the laziest rogue that ever was clothed and fed. So when my time came for the other world, this is the punishment that was laid upon me—to come here and do all this labor every night and then go out and sleep in the cold. It isn't so bad in fine weather, but if you only knew what it is to stand with your head between your legs, facing the storm, from midnight to sunrise on a bleak winter night!"

The boy was moved, and he said, "Is there nothing we could do for your comfort, my poor fellow?"

"Well, I don't know," says the pooka, "but I think a good quilted coat would help to keep the life in me on those long nights."

"Why then, we'd be the ungratefullest of people if we didn't feel for you and give you a coat," said the boy.

So the next night, the boy waited for the pooka again, and delighted the creature by holding up a fine warm horse's coat before him. Between the two of them, they got the pooka's four legs into the coat, and buttoned it down the breast and the belly, and he was so pleased that he walked up to the glass to see how he looked.

"Well," he said at last, "I've a long road to travel tonight. I am much obliged to you and your fellow servants. You have made me happy at last. Goodnight to you."

As he was walking out, the boy cried, "Wait! Sure, you're going too soon. What about the washing and the sweeping?"

"Ah," said the pooka, "you may tell the others that they must now get their turn. My punishment was to last until I was thought worthy of a reward for the way I had done my duty. Now you'll see me no more."

No more they did, and right sorry they were for having been in such a hurry to reward that pooka.

LITTLE WHITE-THORN and THE TALKING BIRD

Brittany

ong ago, when the oak trees used in building the oldest boat at Brest were but acorns, there lived a poor widow whose name was Ninor. Her father had been of noble lineage and had had a large fortune. When he died, he left a manor house, a farm, a mill, and an oven where all the villagers paid to bake their bread. He also left twelve horses and twice as many oxen, twelve cows and ten times that number of sheep, without counting the corn and fine linen.

But as she was a widow, Ninor's brothers would not let her have her share of the inheritance. Perrik, the eldest, kept the manor, the farm, and the horses. Fanche, the second, took the mill and the cows. The third brother, Riwal, had the oxen, the great oven, and the sheep. So nothing was left for Ninor but an old ramshackle cottage on the heath where they usually sent sick animals.

When Ninor was moving her bits of furniture to her poor cottage, Fanche pretended to be sorry for her. "I am going to behave to you as a brother and a Christian," he said. "I have an old black cow which I have never been able to fatten and which hardly gives enough milk to feed a newborn babe. But you may take her with you. White-Thorn can keep her on the heath."

White-Thorn was the widow's daughter. She was nearly eleven years old and was so pale that people called her by the name of the white hedge flower.

So Ninor went away with her little, pale daughter, pulling the cow along with a bit of rope. And when they reached the cottage, Ninor sent the girl and the cow out onto the heath together. Every day and all the day long, White-Thorn stayed there looking after Blackie the cow. She spent her time making crosses out of broom and daisies while she sang a melancholy air. And poor Blackie had a hard enough time finding a little grass between the stones.

One day, White-Thorn noticed a bird perched on one of the flowery crosses she had just stuck in the ground. The bird was chirping and shaking its head. He looked at her as if he wanted to speak. The girl went nearer to the bird and listened carefully, but she could understand nothing. Still, White-Thorn was entranced with the little bird, and she watched it so long that night began to fall. She had forgotten about Blackie. At last the bird flew away, and as White-Thorn followed him with her eyes, she saw that the stars were twinkling in the sky.

Then she looked for Blackie but could not find her. She called, she struck the tufts of broom with her stick, she went down into the hollows where the rainwater had formed little pools, but all in vain. Blackie was not to be found. At last, the child heard her mother calling as if some misfortune had befallen. Frightened, White-Thorn hurried toward her, and at the entrance to the field, on the path leading to their cottage, she saw the widow kneeling near Blackie. The wolves from the forest had gotten her and nothing was left but her bones and horns.

White-Thorn burst into tears and fell on her knees by her mother. At the sight of her daughter's grief, the widow tried to comfort her. "Do not weep for Blackie as if she were a human being, my darling," she said. "Even though the wolves and bad Christians are against us, heaven will have pity on us. Come, help me to pick some firewood and let us go home."

White-Thorn did as her mother said, but the tears trickled down her pale, wan cheeks. "Poor Blackie," she said to herself. "She was no trouble to lead about. She ate anything, and she was beginning to get fat."

That evening, White-Thorn would eat no supper, and during the night she awoke again and again, thinking that she heard Blackie lowing at the door. Finally, just before daybreak, she was convinced she heard the cow just outside in the field, and she ran out into the fields barefoot and in her petticoat. But Blackie was not there. As she came near the heath, however, she beheld the same bird that she had seen before, perched again on the cross of broom. He was singing and seemed to be calling her, but she understood him no better than she had the day before. She was about to run home when she looked down, and saw what she thought was a gold coin lying at her feet. She tried to turn it over with her toe, but it was not a coin. It was the magic herb of gold that you can see only at sunrise if you are barefoot and half-dressed, and if you see it, then the fairies will bestow on you the gift of sight.

And so it was: the moment she touched the herb she understood the language of the birds.

"White-Thorn, I want to do you a good turn," the bird was saying. "White-Thorn, listen to me."

"Who are you?" asked White-Thorn, very much astonished that she could understand the bird.

"I am Robin Redbreast," said the bird, "and each year I am allowed to make a poor girl rich. This time I have chosen you."

"Oh, Robin, Robin," cried White-Thorn, "will I be rich enough to have a shining silver cross with a shining silver chain to go about my neck? And a pair of wooden shoes for my feet as well?"

"You shall have a golden cross and silken shoes," answered the bird.

"And what must I do to have all that, little bird?" asked White-Thorn.

"You must follow me wherever I lead you," Robin said.

"I will do it," said White-Thorn.

And so Robin Redbreast flew off, and White-Thorn went running after him. She followed him across the fields and through the woods until they came to the dunes just opposite the Seven Isles. There the bird stopped.

"Can you see anything below on the beach?" asked Robin.

"Yes," said White-Thorn, "I see a pair of wooden shoes and a wooden staff."

"Put on the shoes and take the staff," said Robin Redbreast.

"I will," said White-Thorn, running down to the beach.

"Now," directed Robin, "you must walk on the sea 'til you reach the first island. Then you must go round it 'til you come to a rock all hidden beneath reeds that are the color of the sea."

"And then what must I do?" asked the girl.

"You must gather the reeds and make a halter."

"That will be easy enough," said White-Thorn.

"And then, with your wooden staff, you must strike the rock as hard as you can until it cracks open."

That did not seem so easy, but White-Thorn did as she was told and carried out all the bird's instructions. With the magic shoes she walked on the sea to the first island. She went round it until she came to the rock with the sea-green reeds. With these she made a halter, as the bird had directed. Then with her wooden staff, she struck the rock, as hard as she could.

Instantly it cracked open like an egg, and out of it clambered a cow with skin as smooth as a maiden's cheek, and eyes as soft as the light of dawn. She was very gentle, and White-Thorn, delighted, put the halter on her and led her over the water, then through the woods, and then over the fields, and across the heath until they reached the widow's cottage.

When Ninor saw the cow, she was as happy as she had been sad before. But she was happier still when she milked the cow, for the milk flowed like the water of a spring. Ninor filled all her pots and pans, then she filled her wooden bowls, then her crocks and then her churns, yet still the milk flowed on. It seemed as if the beautiful Sea-Cow, for that is what the talking bird had named her, had milk for all the babes in Brittany.

Soon everyone was gossiping about the widow's cow, and people came from far and near to look upon her. The richest farmers offered to buy Sea-Cow, and each offered a higher price than the others.

At last Perrik came and said to his sister, "If you are a Christian, you will remember that I am your brother and you will let me have the first offer. Let me have Sea-Cow, and in exchange I'll give you nine of my own cows."

"Sea-Cow is not only worth nine cows," answered the widow Ninor, "she is worth all the cows that are grazing in the highlands and the lowlands. Thanks to her I shall be able to sell milk in all the marketplaces from Dinan to Carhaix."

"Very well," said Perrik, "give her to me, sister, and I will give you our father's farm where you were born, with all the fields and ploughs and horses belonging to it."

Ninor accepted Perrik's offer. So they all went to the farm, and, after Ninor had dug up a clump of earth in each field, drunk a cup of water from the well, lighted a fire on the hearth, and cut a tuft of hair from each of the horses' tails to prove she had become the owner of all these things, she gave Sea-Cow to her brother Perrik. And Perrik led the cow away to a house he had in another quarter of that country.

Little White-Thorn cried when she saw her dear Sea-Cow led away, and she was sad all that day. When night fell she went into the stable to put hay in the mangers. The horses seemed to look at her with sympathy.

"Alas," she sighed, "why is Sea-Cow not here, too?"

Hardly had she spoken when she heard a gentle lowing, and, as she had stepped on the golden herb and knew the language of animals, she understood these words: "Little Mistress, here I am again."

Very much astonished, White-Thorn turned quickly. Right behind her stood Sea-Cow! "Oh, Sea-Cow!" cried the girl. "Who brought you here?"

"I do not belong to your wicked uncle Perrik," said Sea-Cow, "because I cannot belong to anyone."

"But then," said little White-Thorn, "my mother will have to give back the farmhouse, the fields, and the horses."

"Not at all," answered Sea-Cow, "for they were hers by right. Her brother took them from her unjustly when your grandfather died."

"But my uncle Perrik will come to look for you here," said White-Thorn.

"I will tell you what to do," Sea-Cow said. "First, go and pick three verbena leaves."

White-Thorn ran off and quickly returned with the three leaves.

"Now," said Sea-Cow, "rub me with those leaves from my ears to my tail, and whisper softly three times, 'Saint Ronan of Hibernia, Saint Ronan of Hibernia, Saint Ronan of Hibernia'!"

White-Thorn did as she was told, and as she whispered for the third time, Sea-Cow was transformed into a horse. The girl was wonderstruck.

"Now," said the horse, "your uncle Perrik will not know me. My name is no longer Sea-Cow, but Sea-Horse."

When the widow heard what had happened, she was delighted. The very next day she hastened to try her fine new horse. She loaded her back with corn to take to the market. And you can imagine her surprise when she saw Sea-Horse's back growing longer and longer the more she piled on the sacks of corn, so that she alone could carry as many sacks as all the horses in the parish put together.

You may be sure that the news of it soon spread abroad. When Ninor's brother Fanche heard of it, he came to the farm and asked his sister if she would sell him the horse. She refused until he proposed to give her in exchange the mill and all the pigs he was fattening. So the bargain was struck. And Ninor took possession of the mill as she had of the farm, and then let her brother lead Sea-Horse away.

The very next evening the horse was home again. And again White-Thorn picked three verbena leaves and rubbed her from her ears to her tail, repeating the words "Saint Ronan of Hibernia" three times. No sooner had she done so than the horse changed into a sheep. Instead of white wool, she was covered with scarlet wool as long as hemp and as soft as flax. Sea-Horse was now Sea-Lamb. White-Thorn was delighted and called her mother, who came into the stable to admire this new miracle.

"Go and fetch the shepherd's shears," she said to White-Thorn. "The poor dear beast is weighed down with such a heavy fleece."

But when she tried to shear Sea-Lamb, the wool grew again as fast as she cut it off, so that this sheep alone was worth all the flocks on the mountains.

Now Ninor's third brother, Riwal, happened to be passing by, and he saw what was happening. He at once offered to exchange his oxen, his heaths, and all his sheep for Sea-Lamb. So the widow gave Riwal the sheep. But as he was leading Sea-Lamb away along the shore, suddenly she threw herself into the waves. She swam to the smallest of the Seven Isles, the rock opened to let her pass and closed again, and she was gone.

This time White-Thorn waited in vain for her to come home. She came back neither that day nor the next day, nor ever again. So the girl ran off to the hawthorn bush to look for the talking bird, and there he was singing away as before.

"I was expecting you," said the talking bird. "Sea-Lamb has gone and will never return. Your wicked uncles are punished as they deserved, and now you are an heiress. You are rich enough to wear a golden cross and silken shoes, as I promised you. Now my work is done and I shall fly away. Always remember that you were once poor and that it was a little wild bird that made you rich."

And so the talking bird spread his wings and flew away. White-Thorn never saw him again. But out of gratitude, she was always kind to animals, especially to wild birds, and she always gave to the poor.

THE GIANT'S STAIRS

Ireland

n the road between Passage and Cork, there is an old mansion called Ronayne's Court. It was there that Maurice Ronayne and his wife, Margaret Gould, kept house, and their arms are still carved on the old chimneypiece. They were a mighty worthy couple but had only one son, who was called Philip.

Immediately upon first smelling the cold air of this world, the child sneezed, which was naturally taken to be a good sign of his having a clear head. The subsequent rapidity of his learning was truly amazing, for on the very first day a primer was put into his hands, he tore out the A, B, C page and destroyed it, as a thing quite beneath his notice. No wonder, then, that both father and mother were proud of their heir, who gave such indisputable proofs of genius.

One morning, when he was just seven years old, however, Master Phil went missing, and no one could tell what had become of him. Servants were sent in all directions to seek him, on horseback and on foot, but they returned without any tidings of the boy, whose disappearance altogether was most unaccountable. A large reward was offered, but it produced them no intelligence, and years rolled away without Mr. and Mrs. Ronayne having obtained any satisfactory account of the fate of their lost child.

Nearby the mansion lived one Robin Kelly, a blacksmith who served the Ronayne family, and who had been a great friend to young Master Phil. He was a handyman, and his abilities were held in much estimation by the lads and the lasses of the neighborhood, including the young boy. For besides making plough irons and shoeing horses, which he did to great perfection, he interpreted dreams for the young folk, sang "Arthur O'Bradley" at weddings, and was so good-natured a fellow that he was known by half the county.

Now it happened that Robin had a dream himself, and young Philip appeared to him in it. Robin thought he saw the boy mounted upon a beautiful white horse, telling him how he was made a page to the giant Mahon MacMahon, who had carried him off, and who held his court in the hard heart of the rock. "The seven years—my time of service—are clean out, Robin," said the boy, "and if you release me this night, I will be the making of you for ever after."

"And how will I know," said Robin—cunning enough, even in his sleep—"that this is not simply a dream?"

"Take this," said the boy, "for a token." And at that word, the white horse struck out with one of his hind legs, and gave poor Robin such a kick in the forehead that, thinking he was a dead man, he roared as loud as he could after his brains, and woke up, calling a thousand murders. He found himself in bed, but he had the mark of the blow, the regular print of a horseshoe, upon his forehead as red as blood. Robin Kelly, who never before found himself puzzled at the dream of any other person, did not know what to think of his own.

Robin was well acquainted with the Giant's Stairs. They consist of great masses of rock, which, piled one above another, rise like a flight of steps from very deep water, and up the bold cliff of Carrigmahon. Nor are they badly suited for stairs to those who have legs of sufficient length to stride over a moderate-sized house, or to clear the space of a mile in a hop, a step, and a jump. Both these feats the giant MacMahon was said to have performed in the days of old, and the common tradition of the country said that he dwelled still within the cliff up whose side the stairs led.

Such was the impression that the dream made on Robin, that he determined to put truth to the test. It occurred to him, however, before setting out on this adventure, that a plough iron would be no bad companion. He knew from experience that it was an excellent knockdown argument, having on many occasions settled a little disagreement very quietly. So, putting one on his shoulder, off he marched in the cool of the night.

He walked all the way to the harbor. There, he knocked on the door of an old friend of his, Tom, who on hearing Robin's dream promised him the use of his skiff and, moreover, offered to assist in rowing it to the foot of the Giant's Stairs.

So together they embarked. It was a beautiful, still night, and the little boat glided swiftly along. Only the regular dip of the oars, the distant song of a sailor, and sometimes the voice of a belated traveler at the ferry of Carrigaloe broke the quietness of the land and sea and sky. The tide was in their favor, and in a few minutes Robin and his friend rested on their oars under the dark shadow of the Giant's Stairs.

Robin looked anxiously for the entrance to the giant's palace, which, it was said, might be found by anyone seeking it at midnight. But no such entrance could he see. His impatience had hurried him there before midnight, and after waiting a considerable while in a state of suspense not to be described, Robin, with pure vexation, could not help exclaiming to his companion, "'Tis a pair of fools we are, Tom, for coming here at all on the strength of a dream."

"And whose doing is it," said Tom "but your own?"

At the moment he spoke, they perceived a faint glimmering of light proceeding from the cliff, which gradually increased until a porch big enough for a king's palace unfolded itself almost on a level with the water. They pulled the skiff directly towards the opening, and Robin Kelly, seizing his plough iron, boldly entered with a strong hand and a stout heart.

Wild and strange was that entrance, the whole of which appeared formed of grim and grotesque faces blending so strangely with each other that it was impossible to define any one. The chin of one formed the nose of another; what appeared to be a fixed and stern eye, if dwelled upon, changed into a gaping mouth; and the lines of the lofty forehead grew into a majestic and flowing beard. The more Robin allowed himself to contemplate the forms around him, the more terrific they became, and the stony expression of this crowd of faces assumed a savage ferocity as his imagination converted feature after feature into a different shape and character. At last, he tore his eyes off them and advanced through a dark and devious passage, whilst a deep and rumbling noise sounded, as if the rock was about to close upon him and swallow him up alive forever. Now, indeed, poor Robin felt afraid.

"Robin, Robin," he said to himself, "if you were a fool for coming here, what in the name of fortune are you now?"

But, as before, he had scarcely spoken when he saw a small light twinkling through the darkness in the distance, like a star in the midnight sky. To retreat was out of the question, for there were so many turnings and windings in the passage that he considered he had but little chance of making his way back. Therefore, he proceeded towards the bit of light, and came at last into a spacious chamber, from the roof of which hung the solitary lamp that had guided him. That single lamp afforded Robin abundant light, enough to see several gigantic figures seated around a massive stone table, as if in serious deliberation, although no word disturbed the breathless silence which prevailed. At the head of this table sat Mahon MacMahon himself, whose majestic beard had taken root and in the course of ages grown into the stone slab. He was the first who perceived Robin. Instantly starting up, he drew his long beard from out the huge piece of rock in such haste and with so sudden a jerk that the rock was shattered into a thousand pieces.

"What seek you?" he demanded in a voice of thunder.

"I come," answered Robin, with as much boldness as he could put on, for his heart was almost fainting within him, "I come to claim Philip Ronayne, whose time of service is over this night."

"And who sent you here?" said the giant.

"'Twas of my own accord I came," said Robin.

"Then you must single him out from among my pages," said the giant. "And if you fix the wrong one, your life is the forfeit. Follow me."

He led Robin into a hall of vast extent and filled with lights, along either side of which were rows of beautiful children, all apparently seven years old, and all dressed exactly alike in green.

"Here," said Mahon, "you are free to take Philip Ronayne, if you will. But, remember, I give but one choice."

Robin was sadly perplexed, for there were hundreds upon hundreds of children, and it had been years since he had laid eyes on young Philip. But he walked along the hall as if nothing was the matter, side by side with Mahon, whose great iron dress clanked fearfully at every step, sounding louder than Robin's own sledge when he battered it on his anvil.

They had nearly reached the end of the hall without speaking, when Robin, seeing that the only means he had was to make friends with the giant, determined to try what effect a few soft words might have.

"'Tis a fine, wholesome appearance the poor children carry," remarked Robin, "although they have been here so long, shut out from the fresh air and the blessed light of heaven. 'Tis tenderly your honor must have reared them!"

"Ay," said the giant, "that is true. So give me your hand, for you are, I believe, a very honest fellow for a blacksmith."

Then all the young boys began to whisper amongst themselves, and Robin, looking at the huge hand the giant was offering, suspected a trap.

Therefore, instead of his own hand, he presented his plough iron, which the giant seized and twisted in his grasp round and round again as if it had been a potato stalk.

On seeing this, all the children gave a shout of laughter. In the midst of their mirth Robin thought he heard his name called, and looking around quickly, he put his hand on the shoulder of the boy who, he fancied, had spoken. And he cried out at the same time, "Let me live or die for it, but this is young Phil Ronayne."

"It is Philip Ronayne, happy Philip Ronayne," said his young companions.

In an instant the hall became dark. Crashing noises were heard, and all was in strange confusion. But Robin held fast to the boy, and a moment later found himself lying in the grey dawn of the morning in the carved entranceway again, with the boy clasped in his arm. They scrambled together into the waiting skiff, which Tom began to row away in a hurry. And when Robin looked back over his shoulder at the Giant's Stairs, there was no doorway to be seen.

The story spread soon enough that young Master Phil was returned to his family, and Robin Kelly was he who had rescued him. "Are you quite sure, Robin, it is young Phil Ronayne you have brought back with you?" was the regular question, for although the boy had been seven years away, his appearance was now just the same as on the day he went missing. He had grown neither taller nor older in look, and he spoke of things which had happened before he was carried off as if they had occurred yesterday.

"Am I sure? Well, that's a queer question," was Robin's reply, "seeing the boy has the blue eye of the mother, with the foxy hair of the father, to say nothing of the wart on the right side of his little nose. I recognized him right away myself."

However Robin Kelly may have been questioned, the worthy couple doubted not that he had delivered their child from the power of the giant MacMahon, and the reward they bestowed on him equaled their gratitude.

Philip Ronayne lived to be an old man, and he was remarkable to the day of his death for his skill in working brass and iron. It was believed he had learned this skill during his seven years' apprenticeship to the giant Mahon MacMahon, and he put it to use working in the smithy side by side with Robin Kelly for many years.

THE WITCH of FIFE

Scotland

n the kingdom of Fife, in the days of long ago, there lived an old man and his wife. The old man was a quiet sort, but the old woman was flighty and capricious, and some of the neighbors looked at her askance, and whispered to each other that they sorely feared she was a witch.

Her husband was afraid of it, too, for she had a curious habit of disappearing in the evening and staying out all night, and when she returned in the morning she looked quite white and tired, as if she had been traveling far or working hard. He used to try to watch her carefully, in order to find out where she went or what she did, but he never managed to do so, for she always slipped out of the door when he was not looking, and before he could reach it to follow her, she had vanished utterly.

At last, one day when he could stand the uncertainty no longer, he asked her to tell him straight out whether she was a witch or no. And his blood ran cold when, without the slightest hesitation, she answered that she was, and that if he would promise not to let anyone know, the next time that she went on one of her midnight expeditions she would tell him all about it.

The man promised, and he had not long to wait, for the very next week was the new moon, which, as everybody knows, is the time when witches like to stir abroad. On the first sight of the new moon, his wife vanished and did not return until daybreak next morning.

When he asked her where she had been, she told him, in great glee, how she and four like-minded companions had met at the old Kirk on the moor, and had mounted branches of the green bay tree and stalks of hemlock, which had instantly changed into horses. They had ridden swift as the wind over the country, hunting the foxes, the weasels, and the owls. At last, they had swum in the Forth, and come to the top of Bell Lomond. And there, they had dismounted from their horses and drunk beer that had been brewed in no earthly brewery, out of horn cups that had been fashioned by no mortal hands.

After that, a wee, wee man had jumped up from under a great mossy stone with a tiny set of bagpipes under his arm, and he had piped such wonderful music that, at the sound of it, the very trouts jumped out of the Loch below, the stoats crept out of their holes, and the crows and the herons came and sat on the trees in the darkness to listen. And all the witches had danced until they were so weary that, when the time came for them to mount their steeds again, they could scarce sit on them for fatigue.

The man listened to this long story in silence, shaking his head, and when it was finished, all that he answered was, "And what the better are you for all your dancing? You'd have been a deal more comfortable at home."

At the next new moon, the old wife went off again for the night, and when she returned in the morning she told her husband how, on this occasion, she and her friends had taken cockleshells for boats, and had sailed away over the stormy sea until they reached Norway. There they had mounted invisible horses of wind, and had ridden and ridden over mountains, glens, and glaciers until they reached the land of the Lapps lying under its mantle of snow. And there, all the elves and fairies and mermaids of the north were holding festival with warlocks and brownies and pixies and even the phantom hunters themselves, who are never looked upon by mortal eyes. The witches from

Fife held festival with them and danced, feasted, and sang. And, what was of more consequence, they learned from them certain wonderful words which, when uttered, would bear them through the air and would undo all bolts and bars, and so gain them admittance to any place whatsoever they wanted to be. After that they had come home again, delighted with the knowledge which they had acquired.

"What took you to such a land as that?" asked the old man, with a contemptuous grunt. "You would have been a sight warmer in your bed."

But when his wife returned from her next adventure, he showed a little more interest in her doings. For she told him how she and her friends had met in one of their cottages and, having heard that the Lord Bishop of Carlisle had some very rare wine in his cellar, had placed their feet on the crook from which the pot hung, and had pronounced the magic words which they had learned from the elves of Lapland. And, lo and behold, they flew up the chimney like whiffs of smoke and sailed through the air like little wreaths of cloud, and in less time than it takes to tell, they landed at the Bishop's palace at Carlisle. The bolts and the bars flew loose before them, and they went down to his cellar and sampled his wine and were back in Fife as fine, sober, old women by cockcrow.

When he heard this, the old man started from his chair in earnest, for he loved good wine above all things, and it was but seldom that it came his way. "By my troth, but you are a wife to be proud of!" he cried. "Tell me the words, woman! I will go and sample his Lordship's wine for myself."

But his wife shook her head. "No, no! I cannot do that," she said, "for if I did, and you told it over again, it would turn the whole world upside down. For everybody would be leaving their own lawful work and flying about the world after other folk's business and other folk's dainties. So just bide content. You get on fine with the knowledge you already possess."

Although the old man tried to persuade her with all the soft words he could think of, she would not tell him her secret. But he was a sly old man, and the thought of the Bishop's wine gave him no rest. So night after night, he went and hid by the other old woman's cottage in the hope that his wife and her friends would meet there. And at last his trouble was rewarded. For one evening, the five old women assembled. In low tones and with chuckles of laughter, they recounted all that had befallen them in Lapland. Then, running to the fireplace one after another, they climbed on a chair and put their feet on the sooty crook. Then they repeated the magic words, and presto! They were up the chimney and away before the old man could draw his breath.

"I can do that, too," he said to himself, and he crawled out of his hiding place and ran to the fire. He put his foot on the crook and repeated the words. Up the chimney he went, and he flew through the air after his wife and her companions as if he had been a warlock born.

As witches are not in the habit of looking over their shoulders, they never noticed that he was following them until they reached the Bishop's palace and went down into his cellar. Then, when they found that he was with them, they were not too well pleased.

However, there was no help for it, and they settled down to enjoy themselves. They tapped this cask of wine and they tapped that, drinking a little of each but not too much, for they were cautious old women and knew that if they wanted to get home before cockcrow, it behooved them to keep their heads clear.

But the old man was not so wise. He sipped and he sipped, until at last he became quite drowsy, lay down on the floor, and fell fast asleep. His wife, seeing this, thought that she would teach him a lesson not to be so curious in the future. So, when she and her four friends thought that it was time to be gone, she departed without waking him.

He slept peacefully for some hours, until two of the Bishop's servants, coming down to the cellar to draw wine for their master's table, almost fell over him in the darkness. Greatly astonished at his presence there, for the cellar door was locked, they dragged him up to the light, shook him and cuffed him, and asked him how he came to be there.

The poor old man was so confused at being awakened in this rough way, and his head seemed to whirl round so fast, that all he could stammer out was that he came from Fife and that he had traveled on the midnight wind. As soon as they heard that, the servants cried out that he was a warlock, and they dragged him before the Bishop. And, as bishops in those days had a holy horror of warlocks and witches, he ordered the man to be burned alive.

When the sentence was pronounced, you may be very sure that the poor old man wished with all his heart that he had stayed quietly at home in bed and never hankered after the Bishop's wine. But it was too late to wish for that now, for the servants dragged him out into the courtyard, put a chain round his waist, fastened it to a great iron stake, piled bundles of wood round his feet, and set them alight.

As the first tiny little tongue of flame crept up, the old man thought that his last hour had come. But when he thought that, he forgot completely that his wife was a witch.

For, just as the flames began to singe his breeches, there was a swish and a flutter in the air, and a great grey bird with outstretched wings appeared in the sky, swooped down suddenly, and perched for a moment on the old man's shoulder. It gave one fierce croak and flew away again, but to the old man's ears that croak was the sweetest music that he had ever heard.

For to him it was not the croak of an earthly bird, but the voice of his wife whispering the magic words to him. When he heard them he jumped for joy, for he knew that they were words of deliverance. He shouted them aloud, his chains fell off, and he mounted in the air—up and up—while the onlookers watched him in awestruck silence.

He flew right away to the kingdom of Fife, and when he found himself once more safely at home, you may be very sure that he never tried to find out his wife's secrets again, but left her to her own devices.

2

THE SEA

ASSIPATTLE and the
MESTER STOORWORM

—

Scotland

n far bygone days, in the north of Scotland, there lived a well-to-do farmer who had seven sons. And the youngest of them bore a very curious name: people called him Assipattle, which means "he who grovels among the ashes."

Perhaps Assipattle deserved his name, for he was a lazy boy. He never did any work on the farm as his brothers did, but rather ran about outdoors with ragged clothes, unkempt hair, and a mind full of wondrous stories of trolls and giants, elves and goblins. When the sun was hot in the long summer afternoons, when the bees droned drowsily and even the tiny insects seemed almost asleep, the boy was content to throw himself down on the ash heap and lie there, lazily letting the ashes run through his fingers (as one might play with sand on the seashore), basking in the sunshine, and telling stories to himself.

His brothers, working hard in the fields, would point to him with mocking fingers, laugh, and say to each other how well the name suited him, and how little use he was in the world. When they came home from their work, they would push Assipattle about and tease him. And his mother would make him sweep the floor, draw water from the well, fetch peats from the peat stack, and do all the little odd jobs that nobody else would do.

One day, a rider came riding past the farm in hot haste, bearing the most terrible tidings. The evening before, some fishermen had caught sight of the Mester Stoorworm, which, as everyone knows, was the largest and the first and the greatest of all sea serpents.

The fishermen had seen this fearsome monster with its head turned towards the mainland. They had, moreover, seen it open up its mouth and yawn horribly, as if to show that it was hungry and that, if it were not fed, it would kill every living thing upon the land, both man and beast. For 'twas well known that the Mester Stoorworm's breath was so poisonous that it consumed everything in its path, like a burning fire. If it pleased the awful creature to lift its head and put forth its noxious breath over the country, then in a few weeks the fair land would be turned into a region of desolation.

As you may imagine, everyone was almost paralyzed with terror at this awful news. The king called a solemn meeting of all his counsellors, and asked them if they could devise any way of warding off the danger. And for three whole days they sat in council, these grave, bearded men. Many were the suggestions which were made, and many the words of wisdom which were spoken. But, alas! No one was wise enough to think of a way in which the Mester Stoorworm might be driven back from their shores.

At last, at the end of the third day, when everyone had given up hope of finding a remedy, the door of the council chamber opened and the queen appeared.

Now the queen was the king's second wife, and she was not a favorite in the kingdom, for she was a proud, insolent woman, who did not behave kindly to her stepdaughter, Princess Gemdelovely, and who spent much more of her time in the company of a great and dreaded sorcerer than in the company of her husband, the king. So the sober counsellors looked at her disapprovingly as she came boldly into the council chamber and addressed them thus:

"You think that you are brave men and strong and fit to be the protectors of the people. And so it may be, when it is mortals whom you are called on to face. But you are no match for the foe that now threatens our land. Before him your weapons are but as straw. 'Tis not through strength of arm, but through sorcery that he will be overcome. So listen to my words, and take counsel with the great sorcerer, from whom nothing is hid, but who knows all the mysteries of the earth and of the air and of the sea."

Now the king and his counsellors liked not this advice, for they hated the sorcerer, but they were at their wits' end, and knew not to whom they should turn for help. So they had no choice but to do as she said and summon the wizard before them.

When he obeyed the summons and appeared in their midst, they liked him none the better for his looks. He was long and thin, with a beard that came down to his knee and a face the color of mortar, as if he had always lived in darkness and had been afraid to look on the sun. But there was no help to be found in any other man, so they laid the case before him and asked him what they should do. He answered coldly that he would think the matter over and come again to the assembly the following day to give them his advice.

And his advice, when they heard it the next day, was enough to turn their hair white with horror.

For the sorcerer said that the only way to satisfy the monster was to feed it every Saturday with seven young maidens, the fairest who could be found. If, after three Saturdays, this remedy did not succeed in mollifying the Stoorworm and inducing him to depart, there was but one other measure that he could suggest. But that was so horrible and dreadful that he would not rend their hearts by mentioning it in the meantime.

So on that very Saturday, seven bonnie, innocent maidens were bound hand and foot and laid on a rock which ran into the sea. Then the monster stretched out his long, jagged tongue and swept them into his mouth while all the rest of the folk looked on from the top of a high hill.

"Is there no other way," cried the women, "no other way than this to save the land?"

But the men only groaned and shook their heads. "No other way," they answered. "No other way."

Then suddenly a boy's indignant voice rang out among the crowd. "Is there no one who would fight that monster and kill him and save the lass-ies? I would do it. I am not afraid of the Mester Stoorworm."

It was Assipattle who spoke, and everyone looked at him in amazement as he stood staring at the great sea serpent, his fingers twitching with rage, and his great blue eyes glowing with pity and indignation.

"The poor bairn's mad. The sight has turned his head," they whispered one to another. And they would have crowded round him to pet and com-fort him, but his elder brother came and gave him a heavy clout on the side of his head.

"You fight the Stoorworm!" he cried contemptuously. "A likely story! Go home to your ash pit and stop speaking nonsense." And taking Assi-pattle's arm, he drew him away.

TWO MORE WEEKS PASSED, and on every Saturday, seven lassies were thrown to the Stoorworm. But still the monster lingered by the shore and showed no signs of leaving. So the elders met once more, and, after long consultation, summoned the sorcerer again to ask what his other remedy was. "For, by our troth," said they, "it cannot be worse than that which we are practicing now."

But in fact the new remedy was even more dreadful than the old. For the cruel queen hated her stepdaughter, Gemdelovely, and the wicked sor-cerer knew that she did. So he stood up in the council and, pretending to be very sorry, said that the only thing to be done was to give Princess Gemdelovely to the Stoorworm, and then it would surely depart.

When he said this, a terrible stillness fell upon the council and everyone covered his face with his hands, for no man dared look at the king. But although his dear daughter was the apple of his eye, the king was a just and righteous monarch, and he felt that it was not right to force other fathers to part with their daughters while sparing his. So, after he had spoken with the princess, he stood up before the elders and declared, with trembling voice, that both he and she were ready to make the sacrifice.

"She is my only child," he said. "Yet it seems good to both of us that she should lay down her life, if by so doing she may save the land that she loves so well."

So, amid heavy sobs, the chief of the council pronounced the princess's doom. But as he did so, one of the king's knights stepped forward.

"Nature teaches us that each beast has a tail," he said, "and the doom just pronounced is indeed a venomous beast. So, if I had my way, the tail of this beast should be that if the Mester Stoorworm does not depart, and that right speedily, after devouring the princess, then the next thing offered to him should be no tender young maiden, but that tough, lean old sorcerer."

At his words there was such a great shout of approval that the wicked sorcerer seemed to shrink within himself, and his pale face grew paler than it was before.

Now, three weeks were allowed before offering the princess to the Stoorworm, so that the king might send ambassadors to all the neighboring kingdoms. The ambassadors proclaimed that, if any champion would come forward and drive away the Stoorworm, he should have the princess for his wife, and with her, the kingdom and the king's prized sword, which was called Sickersnapper. The news spread over the length and breadth of the land, and everyone mourned for the fate that was likely to befall

Princess Gemdelovely. The farmer and his wife and their sons mourned also—all but Assipattle, who sat amongst the ashes and said nothing.

Meanwhile, there was a fine stir among all the young gallants, for it seemed but a little thing to slay a sea monster. And a beautiful wife, a fertile kingdom, and a trusty sword are not to be won every day. So six-and-thirty champions arrived at the king's palace, each hoping to gain the prize. But when the king sent them all out to look at the giant Stoorworm lying in the sea with its enormous mouth open, twelve of them were seized with sudden illness, and twelve of them were so afraid that they took to their heels and ran and never stopped until they reached their own countries. So only twelve returned to the king's palace, but they were so downcast that they had no spirit left in them at all, and the three weeks passed without any of them daring to try to kill the Stoorworm.

On the night before the day on which the princess was to be sacrificed, the king went to the great hall and opened the chest in which he kept all the things that he treasured most. The old monarch undid the iron bolts with trembling fingers, lifted the lid, and took out the wondrous sword Sickersnapper.

His trusty knight, who had stood by him in a hundred fights, watched him with pitying eyes and said, "Why lift you out the sword when your fighting days are done? 'Tis time to leave such work to younger men."

The old king turned on him angrily. "Wheest," he cried. "Do you think that I can see my only bairn devoured by a monster, and not lift a finger to try and save her when no one else will? I tell you—and I will swear it with my two thumbs crossed on Sickersnapper—that both the sword and I will be destroyed before so much as one of her hairs be touched. So go and order my boat to be ready, with the sail set and the prow pointed out to sea. I will go myself and fight the Stoorworm."

Meanwhile, at the farm, everybody went to bed early, for next morning the whole family was to set out early to go to the top of the hill near the sea and see the princess eaten by the Stoorworm. All except Assipattle, who was to be left at home to herd the geese. The lad was so vexed at this that he could not sleep. As he lay tossing and tumbling about in his corner among the ashes, he heard his father and mother having an argument.

"'Tis such a long way to the hill overlooking the sea, I fear me I shall never walk it," said his mother. "I think I had better bide at home."

"Nay," replied his father, "that would be a bonny-like thing, when all the countryside is to be there. You will ride behind me on my good mare, Go-Swift."

"I do not care to trouble you so," said his mother, "for methinks you do not love me as you once did."

"What makes you think I have ceased to love you?" cried his father impatiently.

"Because you will no longer tell me your secrets. To begin with, think of this very horse, Go-Swift. For five long years, I have been begging you to tell me how it is that, when you ride her, she flies faster than the wind, but if any other man mounts her, she walks along like a broken-down nag."

Assipattle's father laughed. "Well, since my silence has vexed your heart, I will tell you. When I want Go-Swift to stand, I give her one clap on the left shoulder. When I would have her go like any other horse, I give her two claps on the right. But when I want her to fly like the wind, I whistle through the windpipe of a goose. And, as I never ken when I want her to gallop like that, I always keep the goose thrapple in the left hand pocket of my coat."

"So that is how you manage the beast," said the farmer's wife, in a satisfied tone, "and that is what becomes of all my goose thrapples!"

Assipattle was not tumbling about in the ashes now; he was sitting up in the darkness, with glowing cheeks and sparkling eyes. His opportunity had come at last, and he knew it. He waited patiently until his parents were asleep. Then he crept over to where his father's clothes lay, took the goose thrapple out of the pocket of his coat, and slipped noiselessly out of the house. He saddled and bridled Go-Swift, threw a halter around her neck, and led her to the stable door.

The mare pranced and reared and plunged, but Assipattle, knowing his father's secret, clapped her once on the left shoulder, and she stood as still as a stone. Then he mounted her and gave her two claps on the right shoulder, and the good horse trotted off briskly, giving a loud neigh as she did so.

The sound, ringing out in the stillness of the night, roused the household, and Assipattle's father and six brothers came tumbling down the wooden stairs, shouting to one another in confusion that someone was stealing Go-Swift.

The farmer was the first to reach the door, and when he saw, in the starlight, the vanishing form of his favorite steed, he cried at the top of his voice, "Stop, thief! Go-Swift, whoa!"

When Go-Swift heard that, she pulled up in a moment. All seemed lost, for the farmer and his sons could run very fast indeed. But Assipattle remembered the goose thrapple, and he pulled it out of his pocket and whistled through it. In an instant the mare bounded forward, swift as the wind, and was over the hill and out of reach of her pursuers before they had taken ten steps more.

Day was dawning when the lad came within sight of the sea, and there in front of him lay the enormous monster whom he had come so far to slay. But Assipattle was not afraid, for he had the heart of a hero underneath his tattered garments. "I must be cautious," he said to himself, "and do by my wits what I cannot do by my strength."

He watched the Stoorworm intently for a little while, and he noticed that the terrible monster yawned occasionally, as if longing for its weekly feast. And as it yawned, a great flood of seawater went down its throat and came out again at its huge gills.

Then Assipattle climbed down from his seat on Go-Swift's back and tethered the horse to a tree. He walked on along the coast until he came to a little cottage on the edge of a wood. The door was not locked, so he entered and found its occupant, an old woman, fast asleep in bed. He did not disturb her, but he took down an iron pot from the shelf and examined it closely.

"This will serve my purpose," he said, "and surely the old dame would not grudge it if she knew it was to save the princess's life."

Then he lifted a glowing brick of peat from the smoldering fire, put it in the iron pot, and went on his way.

Down at the water's edge, he found the king's boat guarded by a single boatman, with its sails set and its prow turned in the direction of the Mester Stoorworm.

"It's a cold morning," said Assipattle. "Are you not well-nigh frozen sitting there? If you will come on shore to run about and warm yourself, I will get into the boat and guard it 'til you return."

"A likely story," replied the man. "And what would the king say if he were to come, as I expect every moment he will do, and find me playing on the sand and his good boat left to a smatchet like you? He would have my head."

"As you like," said Assipattle carelessly, beginning to search among the rocks. "In the meantime, I must be looking for some mussels to roast for my breakfast."

He gathered some mussels, and then he began to make a hole in the sand to put the live peat in. The boatman watched him curiously, for he was beginning to feel hungry.

Presently the lad gave a wild shriek and jumped high in the air. "Gold, gold!" he cried. "Who would have looked to find gold here?"

This was too much for the boatman. Forgetting all about his head and the king, he jumped out of the boat and, pushing Assipattle aside, began to scrape among the sand with all his might. While he was doing so, Assipattle seized his pot, jumped into the boat, and pushed her off, and he was half a mile out to sea before the outwitted man noticed what he was about.

Of course, he was very angry, but the old king was angrier still when he came down to the shore, attended by his nobles and carrying the great sword Sickersnapper, in the vain hope that he might be able in some way to defeat the monster and save his daughter. To make such an attempt was beyond his power now that his boat was gone. So he could only stand on the shore, along with the fast assembling crowd of his subjects, and watch what would befall.

What he saw was Assipattle lowering his sail and pointing the prow of his boat straight at the Mester Stoorworm's mouth, so that the next time it yawned, he and his boat were sucked right in and went straight down its throat. On and on the boat floated into the dark regions of the creature's body. But as it went the water grew less, pouring out of the Stoorworm's gills, until at last the boat stuck, as it were, on dry land. And Assipattle jumped out, his pot in his hand, and began to explore.

Presently, he came to the huge creature's liver, and having heard that the liver of a fish is full of oil, he made a hole in it and put in the live peat.

Woe's me, but there was a conflagration! Assipattle just got back to his boat in time, for the Mester Stoorworm, in its convulsions, threw the boat right out of its mouth again, and it was flung up high and dry on the hill above the sea.

The commotion in the sea was terrible. The distressed creature tossed itself to and fro, twisting and writhing, and as it tossed its awful head out of the water, its tongue fell out and struck the earth with such force that it made a great dent in it, into which the sea rushed. And that dent formed the crooked straits which now divide Denmark from Norway and Sweden. Then some of its teeth fell out and rested in the sea, and became the islands that we now call the Orkney Isles. And a little afterwards some more teeth dropped out, and they became what we now call the Shetland Isles.

After that, the creature twisted itself into a great lump and finally died, and this lump became the island of Iceland; and the fire which Assipattle had kindled with his live peat still burns on underneath it, which is why there are mountains that throw out fire in that chilly land.

When at last it was plain to see that the Mester Stoorworm was dead, the king could scarcely contain himself with joy. He put his arms around Assipattle's neck, and kissed his brow, and called him his son. He took off his own royal mantle and put it on the lad, and girded his good sword Sickersnapper round his waist. Then he called his daughter to him and put her hand in Assipattle's, and he declared that when the right time came, they should be married and rule over all the kingdom.

The whole company rejoiced, and Assipattle rode on Go-Swift by the princess's side as they returned with great joy to the palace. As they neared the gate, one of the princess's maids ran out to meet them, and whispered something in the princess's ear. The princess's face grew dark, and she turned her horse's head and rode back to where her father was. She told him the words that the maid had spoken, and when he heard them his face, too, grew as black as thunder.

For the matter was this: The cruel queen, full of joy at the thought that she was to be rid of her stepdaughter, had been making love to the wicked sorcerer all morning in the old king's absence.

"He shall be killed at once," cried the monarch. "Such behavior cannot be overlooked."

"You will have much ado to find him, Your Majesty," said the maid, "for 'tis more than an hour since he and the queen fled together on the fleetest horses that they could find in the stables."

"But I can find him," cried Assipattle, and he went off like the wind on his good horse Go-Swift.

It was not long before he came within sight of the fugitives, and he drew his sword and shouted at them to stop. They heard the shout and turned round, but they both laughed aloud in derision when they saw that it was only the boy who groveled in the ashes who pursued them.

"The insolent brat! I will cut off his head for him and teach him a lesson," cried the sorcerer, and he rode boldly back to meet Assipattle. For although he was no fighter, his body was enchanted and no ordinary weapon could harm him.

But he did not count on Assipattle having the great Sickersnapper. Before this magic weapon the sorcerer was powerless. With one thrust, the young lad ran it through his body as easily as if he had been any ordinary man, and he fell from his horse, dead.

The queen was brought before the council, judged, and condemned to be shut up in a high tower for the remainder of her life. As for Assipattle, he was married to Princess Gemdelovely when they were old enough, and there was great feasting and rejoicing. And when the old king died, they ruled the kingdom for many a long year.

THE SEAL CATCHER
and THE SELKIES

———

Scotland

 nce upon a time, there was a man who lived not far from the very north of Scotland. He dwelled in a little cottage by the seashore and made his living by catching seals and selling their fur. He earned a good deal of money in this way, for these creatures used to come out of the sea in large numbers and lie on the rocks near his house, basking in the sunshine, so that it was not difficult to creep up behind them and kill them.

Some of those seals were larger than others, and the country people used to call them selkies and whisper that they were not seals at all, but mermen and merwomen who came from a country of their own, far down under the ocean, and who assumed this strange disguise in order to pass through the water and come up to breathe the air of this earth of ours. But the seal catcher only laughed, and said that those seals were the ones most worth killing, for their skins were so big that he got an extra price for them.

Now it chanced that one day, as he crept up to and stabbed one of these particularly large seals with his hunting knife, the creature gave a loud cry of pain and slipped off the rock into the sea. It disappeared under the water, carrying the knife along with it.

The seal catcher, much annoyed at his clumsiness and also at the loss of his knife, went home to dinner in a very downcast frame of mind. On his way he met a horseman, who was so tall and strange-looking and who rode on such a gigantic horse, that the seal catcher stopped and looked at him in astonishment, wondering who he was and from what country he came.

The stranger stopped as well and asked him his trade. On hearing that he was a seal catcher, he immediately ordered a great number of seal skins. The seal catcher was delighted, for such an order meant a large sum of money to him. But his face fell when the horseman added that it was absolutely necessary that the skins should be delivered that evening.

"I cannot do it," said the seal catcher in a disappointed voice, "for the seals will not come back to the rocks again until tomorrow morning."

"I can take you to a place where there are any number of seals," answered the stranger, "if you will mount behind me on my horse and come with me."

The seal catcher agreed to this and climbed up behind the rider. Then the rider shook his bridle rein, and off the great horse galloped at such a pace that the seal catcher had much ado to keep his seat. On and on they went, flying like the wind, until at last they came to the edge of a huge precipice, the face of which went sheer down to the sea. Here the mysterious horseman pulled up his steed with a jerk.

"Get off now," he said shortly.

The seal catcher did as he was bid, and when he found himself safe on the ground, he peeped cautiously over the edge of the cliff, to see if there were any seals lying on the rocks below. To his astonishment, he saw no rocks, only the blue sea, which came right up to the foot of the cliff.

"Where are the seals that you spoke of?" he asked anxiously, wishing that he had never set out on such a rash adventure.

"You will see presently," answered the stranger, who was attending to his horse's bridle.

The seal catcher was now thoroughly frightened, for he felt sure that some evil was about to befall him, and in such a lonely place he knew that it would be useless to cry out for help. And it seemed as if his fears would prove only too true, for the next moment, the stranger's hand was laid upon his shoulder, and he felt himself being hurled bodily over the cliff. Then he fell with a splash into the sea.

He thought that his last hour had come, and he wondered how anyone could work such a deed of wrong upon an innocent man. But, to his astonishment, he found that some change must have passed over him, for instead of being choked by the water, he could breathe quite easily. He and his companion, who was still close at his side, seemed to be sinking as quickly down through the sea as they had flown through the air.

Down and down they went, he couldn't tell how far, until at last they came to a huge arched door, which appeared to be made of pink coral studded over with cockleshells. It opened of its own accord, and when they entered, they found themselves in a huge hall, the walls of which were formed of mother-of-pearl, and the floor of which was made of sea sand, smooth, firm, and yellow.

The hall was crowded with occupants, but they were seals, not men, and when the seal catcher turned to his companion to ask him what it all meant, he was aghast to find that the rider, too, had assumed the form of a seal. He was still more aghast when he caught sight of himself in a large mirror that hung on the wall and saw that he also no longer bore the likeness of a man, but was transformed into a nice, hairy, brown seal.

"Ah, woe to me," he said to himself. "For no fault of my own, this artful stranger has laid some baneful charm upon me, and in this awful guise will I remain for the rest of my natural life."

At first none of the huge creatures spoke to him. For some reason or another, they seemed to be very sad. They moved gently about the hall, talking quietly and mournfully to one another, or lay sadly upon the sandy floor, wiping big tears from their eyes with their soft, furry fins. But presently they began to notice him and to whisper to one another. Then his guide moved away from him and disappeared through a door at the end of the hall. When he returned, he held a huge knife in his hand.

"Did you ever see this before?" he asked, holding it out to the unfortunate seal catcher, who, to his horror, recognized his own hunting knife, with which he had struck the seal in the morning, and which had been carried off by the wounded animal.

At the sight of the knife, he fell upon his face and begged for mercy, for he at once came to the conclusion that the inhabitants of the cavern, enraged at the harm which had been wrought upon their comrade, had contrived to capture him and to bring him down to their subterranean abode in order to wreak their vengeance upon him by killing him.

But instead of doing so, they crowded round him, rubbing their soft noses against his fur to show their sympathy, and implored him not to put himself about, for no harm would befall him, and they would love him all their lives long if he would only do what they asked him.

"Tell me what it is," said the seal catcher, "and I will do it, if it lies within my power."

"Follow me," answered his guide, and he led the way to the door through which he had disappeared when he went to seek the knife

The seal catcher followed him. And there, in a smaller room, he found a great brown seal lying on a bed of pale pink seaweed, with a gaping wound in his side.

"That is my father," said his guide, "whom you wounded this morning, thinking that he was one of the common seals who live in the sea, instead of a merman who has speech and understanding as you mortals have. I brought you hither to bind up his wounds, for no other hand than yours can heal him."

"I have no skill in the art of healing," said the seal catcher, astonished at the forbearance of these strange creatures, whom he had so unwittingly wronged. "But I will bind up the wound to the best of my power, and I am only sorry that it was my hands that caused it."

He went over to the bed and, stooping over the wounded seal, washed and dressed the hurt as well as he could. And the touch of his hands appeared to work like magic, for no sooner had he finished, than the wound seemed to deaden and die, leaving only the scar, and the old seal sprang up as well as ever.

Then there was a great rejoicing throughout the whole palace of the seals. They laughed, and they talked, and they embraced each other in their own strange way, crowding round their comrade, and rubbing their noses against his, as if to show him how delighted they were at his recovery. But all this while, the seal catcher stood alone in a corner, his mind filled with dark thoughts. For although he saw now that they had no intention of killing him, he did not relish the prospect of spending the rest of his life in the guise of a seal, fathoms deep under the ocean.

But presently his guide approached him and said, "Now you are at liberty to return home to your wife and children. I will take you to them, but only on one condition."

"And what is that?" asked the seal catcher eagerly, overjoyed at the prospect of being restored safely to the upper world and to his family.

"That you will take a solemn oath never to wound a seal again."

"That will I do right gladly," he replied, for although the promise meant giving up his means of livelihood, he felt that if only he regained his proper shape he could always turn his hand to something else.

So he took the required oath with all due solemnity, holding up his fin as he swore, and all of the other seals crowded round him as witnesses. And a sigh of relief went through the halls when the words were spoken, for he was the most noted seal catcher in the north of Scotland.

Then he bade the strange company farewell and, accompanied by his guide, passed once more through the outer doors of coral and up, and up, and up, through the shadowy green water, until it began to grow lighter and lighter and at last they emerged into the sunshine. Then, with one spring, they reached the top of the cliff, where the great black horse was waiting for them, quietly nibbling the green turf.

When they left the water, their strange disguise dropped from them, and they were now as they had been before, a plain seal catcher and a tall, well-dressed gentleman in riding clothes.

"Get up behind me," said the latter, as he swung himself into his saddle.

The seal catcher did as he was bid, taking tight hold of his companion's coat, for he remembered how nearly he had fallen off on his previous journey.

Then it all happened as it happened before. The bridle was shaken, the horse galloped off, and it was not long before the seal catcher found himself standing in safety before his own garden gate. He held out his hand to say good-bye, but as he did so the stranger pulled out a huge bag of gold and placed it in his hand.

"You have done your part of the bargain, we must do ours," he said. "Men shall never say that we took away an honest man's work without making reparation for it, and here is what will keep you in comfort 'til your life's end."

Then he rode away, and when the astonished seal catcher carried the bag into his cottage and turned the gold out on the table, he found that what the stranger had said was true, and that he would be a rich man for the remainder of his days.

THE SOUL CAGES

——

Ireland

ack Dogherty lived in a remote little cottage by Dunbeg Bay, on the coast of County Clare. Jack was a fisherman, as his father and grandfather before him had been. He lived in just the same spot as them and, like them, lived alone except for his wife. People used to wonder why the Dogherty family was so fond of that wild site, so far away from all humankind, and in the midst of huge shattered rocks, with nothing but the wide ocean to look upon. But they had their own good reasons for it.

The place was just about the only spot on that part of the coast where anybody could well live. There was a neat little creek, where a boat might lie as snug as a puffin in her nest, and out from this creek, a ledge of sunken rocks ran into the sea. Now when the Atlantic was raging with a storm, and a good westerly wind was blowing strong on the coast, many a richly laden ship went to pieces on these rocks; and then the fine bales of cotton, tobacco, and such like things, and the pipes of wine, the puncheons of rum, the casks of brandy, and the kegs of Hollands were swept neatly ashore. So Dunbeg Bay was just like a little estate to the Doghertys.

Not that they weren't kind and humane to a distressed sailor, if ever one had the good luck to get to land. Many a time indeed did Jack put out in his little boat and lend a hand towards bringing the crew from a wreck. But when the ship had gone to pieces and the crew were all lost, who would blame Jack for picking up all he could find?

"And who is the worse of it?" said he. "For as to the king, God bless him, everybody knows he's rich enough already without getting what's floating in the sea."

Jack, though such a hermit, was a good-natured, jolly fellow. No other, sure, could ever have coaxed Biddy Mahony to quit her father's snug and warm house in the middle of the town of Ennis, and to go so many miles off to live among the rocks, with the seals and seagulls for next door neighbors. But Biddy knew that Jack was the man for a woman who wished to be comfortable and happy, for, to say nothing of the fish, Jack had the supplying of half the gentlemen's houses in the country with the wrecks that came into the bay. And she was right in her choice, for no woman ate, drank, or slept better, or made a prouder appearance at chapel on Sundays than Mrs. Dogherty.

Many a strange sight did Jack see on that lonely bit of coast, and many a strange sound did he hear, but nothing daunted him. So far was he from being afraid of merrows, or other such magical beings that dwelled in the sea, that the very first wish of his heart was to meet one of them. Jack had heard that luck had always come out of an acquaintance with the merrows. Therefore, whenever he dimly discerned them moving along the face of the water in their robes of mist, he made directly toward them. But he never could catch up, and many a scolding did Biddy bestow upon Jack for spending his whole day out at sea and bringing home no fish. Little did poor Biddy know the fish Jack was after!

It was rather annoying to Jack that, though living in a place where the merrows were as plenty as lobsters, he never could get a right view of one. What vexed him more was that both his father and grandfather had often seen them. He even remembered hearing when he was a child how his grandfather, who was the first of the family that had settled down at the creek, had been good friends with a merrow. This, however, Jack did not well know how to believe.

Fortune at length began to think it only right that Jack should know as much as his father and grandfather did. Accordingly, one day when he had strolled a little farther than usual along the coast, and was just coming around a point of rock, he saw something like to nothing he had ever seen before. It was perched upon a rock at a little distance out to sea, but as well as he could discern at that distance, it looked green in the body and held, he would have sworn, a cocked hat in its hand.

Jack stood for a good half hour straining his eyes and wondering at it, and all the time the thing did not stir hand or foot. At last, Jack's patience was quite worn out, and he gave a loud whistle and a hail. But the merrow, for that is what it was, started up, put the cocked hat on its head, and dived down headfirst from the rock.

After that day, Jack's curiosity was excited, and he constantly directed his steps towards the point. But he could never get a glimpse of the sea-gentleman with the cocked hat, and with thinking and thinking about the matter, he began at last to fancy he had only been dreaming. One very rough day, however, when the sea was running mountains high, Jack determined to give a look at the merrow's rock (for he had always chosen a fine day before), and then he saw the strange thing cutting capers upon the top of the rock, then diving down, and then coming up and diving down again.

Jack had now only to choose a good blowing day, and he could see the man of the sea as often as he pleased. All this, however, did not satisfy him. He wished now to get acquainted with the merrow. Then one tremendous blustering day, before he got to the point whence he had a view of the merrow's rock, the storm came on so furiously that Jack was obliged to take shelter in one of the caves which are so numerous along the coast. And there, to his astonishment, he saw sitting before him a thing with green hair, long green teeth, a red nose, and pig's eyes. It had a fish's tail, legs with scales on them, and short arms like fins. It wore no clothes, but had the cocked hat under its arm, and seemed to be thinking very seriously about something.

Jack, with all his courage, was a little daunted. But now or never, he thought, so up he went boldly to the cogitating fish man, took off his hat, and made his best bow. "Your servant, sir," said Jack.

"Your servant, kindly, Jack Dogherty," answered the merrow.

"To be sure, then, how well your honor knows my name!" said Jack.

"Is it I not know your name, Jack Dogherty? Why, man, I knew your grandfather long before he was married to Judy Regan, your grandmother! Ah, Jack, Jack, I was fond of that grandfather of yours. He was a mighty worthy man. I never met his match above or below, before or since, for sucking in a shellful of brandy. I hope, my boy," said the old fellow, with a merry twinkle in his eyes, "I hope you're his own grandson!"

"Never fear me for that," said Jack. "If my mother had only reared me on brandy, 'tis myself that would be a sucking infant to this hour!"

"Well, I like to hear you talk so manly. You and I must be better acquainted, if only for your grandfather's sake."

"I'm sure," said Jack, "since your honor lives down under the water, you must be obliged to drink a power to keep any heat in you in such a cruel, damp, cold place. Well, I've often heard of men drinking like fishes. And might I be so bold as to ask where you get the spirits?"

"Where do you get them yourself, Jack?" said the merrow, twitching his red nose between his forefinger and thumb.

"Aha, now I see how it is," said Jack. "But I suppose, sir, your honor has got a fine dry cellar below to keep them in."

"Let me alone for the cellar," said the merrow, with a knowing wink.

"I'm sure," continued Jack, "it must be mighty well worth the looking at."

"You may say that, Jack," said the merrow, "and if you meet me here next Monday, just at this time of the day, we will have a little more talk with one another about the matter."

Jack and the merrow parted the best friends in the world. On Monday they met, and Jack was not a little surprised to see that the merrow had two cocked hats with him, one under each arm.

"Might I take the liberty to ask, sir," said Jack, "why your honor has brought the two hats with you today? You would not, sure, be going to give me one of them to keep for the curiosity of the thing?"

"No, no, Jack," said the merrow. "I don't get my hats so easily, to part with them that way. But I want you to come down and dine with me, and I brought you the hat to dine with."

"Lord bless and preserve us!" cried Jack in amazement. "Would you want me to go down to the bottom of the salt sea ocean? Sure I'd be smothered and choked up with the water, to say nothing of being drowned! And what would poor Biddy do for me, and what would she say?"

"And what matter what she says, you *pinkeen*? Who cares for Biddy's squalling? It's long before your grandfather would have talked in that way. Many's the time he stuck that same hat on his head and dived down boldly after me, and many's the snug bit of dinner and good shellful of brandy he and I have had together below, under the water."

"Is that true, sir?" said Jack. "Why, then, here's neck or nothing!"

"That's your grandfather all over," said the old fellow. "So come along and do as I do."

They both left the cave, walked into the sea, and then swam a piece until they got to the rock. The merrow climbed to the top of it, and Jack followed him. On the far side, it was as straight as the wall of a house, and the sea beneath looked so deep that Jack was almost cowed.

"Now, Jack," said the merrow, "just put this hat on your head, and mind to keep your eyes wide open. Take hold of my tail and follow after me, and you'll see what you'll see."

In he dashed, and in dashed Jack boldly after him. Through the water they went, and Jack thought they'd never stop going. Many a time did he wish himself sitting at home by the fireside with Biddy. Yet where was the use of wishing now, when he was so many miles below the waves of the Atlantic? So he held hard to the merrow's tail, slippery as it was, and at last, to Jack's great surprise, they got out of the water, and he actually found himself on dry land at the bottom of the sea.

They landed just in front of a nice house that was slated very neatly with oyster shells. Jack could hardly speak, what with wonder, and what with being out of breath after traveling so fast through the water. He looked about him and could see no living things except crabs and lobsters, of which there were plenty walking leisurely about on the sand. Overhead, the sea was like a sky, and the fishes like birds swimming about in it.

"Why don't you speak, man?" said the merrow. "I daresay you had no notion that I had such a snug little concern here as this? Are you smothered, or choked, or drowned, or are you fretting after Biddy, eh? Well, come along, and let's see what they've got for us to eat."

Jack really was hungry, and it gave him no small pleasure to perceive a fine column of smoke rising from the chimney, announcing what was going on within. Into the house he followed the merrow, and there he saw a good kitchen, right well provided with everything. There was a noble dresser and plenty of pots and pans, with two young merrows cooking. His host then led him into the dining room, which was furnished shabbily enough. There was not a table or chair in it, but only planks and logs of wood to sit on and eat off. However, there was a good fire blazing upon the hearth—a comfortable sign to Jack.

"Come now, and I'll show you where I keep you-know-what," said the merrow, with a sly look.

Opening a little door, he led Jack into a fine cellar, well-filled with pipes, kegs, hogsheads, and barrels.

"What do you say to that, Jack Dogherty? Eh! Maybe a body can live snug under the water?"

"Never the doubt of that," said Jack, with a smack of his lip.

They went back to the dining room and found dinner laid. There was no tablecloth, to be sure, but what matter? Jack and Biddy did not always have one at home, either. The dinner itself would have been no discredit to the finest house in the country. The choicest of fish, no wonder, was there. Turbots, sturgeons, soles, lobsters, oysters, and twenty other kinds were on the planks at once, along with plenty of the best of foreign spirits. Wine, the old fellow said, was too cold for his stomach.

Jack ate and drank until he could eat no more. Then, taking up a shell of brandy, he said, "Here's to your honor's good health, sir, though, begging you pardon, it's mighty odd that as long as we've been acquainted I don't know your name yet."

"That's true, Jack," replied the merrow. "I never thought of it before, but better late than never. My name's Coomara."

"And a mighty decent name it is," cried Jack, taking another shellful. "Here's to your good health, Coomara, and may you live these fifty years to come!"

"Fifty years!" repeated Coomara. "I'm obliged to you, indeed! If you had said five hundred, it would have been something worth the wishing."

"Well, sir," said Jack, "I suppose you live to a powerful age here under the water! You knew my grandfather, and he's dead and gone better than these sixty years. I'm sure it must be a healthy place to live in."

"No doubt of it. But come, Jack, keep the liquor stirring."

Shell after shell did they empty, and to Jack's exceeding surprise, he found the drink never got into his head, owing, he supposed, to the sea being over them, which kept their noodles cool.

Old Coomara got exceedingly comfortable and sung several songs. But Jack, if his life had depended on it, never could remember more than this:

"Rum fum boodle boo,
Ripple dipple nitty dob;
Dumdoo doodle coo,
Raffle taffle chittiboo!"

At length, Coomara said to Jack, "Now, my dear boy, if you'll follow me, I'll show you my curiosities!"

He opened a little door and led the way into a large room, where Jack saw a great many odds and ends that Coomara had picked up at one time or another. What chiefly took his attention, however, were a great many things like lobster pots ranged on the ground along the wall.

"Well, Jack, how do you like my curiosities?" said old Coo.

"Upon my soul, sir," said Jack, "they're mighty well worth the looking at. But might I make so bold as to ask what these things like lobster pots are?"

"Oh! The Soul Cages, is it?"

"The what, sir?"

"These things here that I keep the souls in."

"Arrah! What souls, sir?" said Jack in amazement. "Sure the fish have no souls in them."

"Oh, no," replied Coo, quite coolly, "that they have not. These are the souls of drowned sailors."

"The Lord preserve us from all harm!" muttered Jack. "How in the world did you get them?"

"Easily enough. I've only, when I see a good storm coming on, to set a couple of dozen of these, and then, when the sailors are drowned and the souls get out of them under the water, the poor things are almost perished to death, not being used to the cold. So they make into my pots for shelter, and then I have them snug and fetch them home and keep them here dry and warm. And is it not well for them, poor souls, to get into such good quarters?"

Jack was so thunderstruck that he did not know what to say, so he said nothing. They went back into the dining room and had a little more brandy, which was excellent, and then, as Jack knew that it must be getting late, and as Biddy might be uneasy, he stood up and said he thought it was time for him to be on the road.

"Just as you like, Jack," said Coo, "but take another drink before you go. You've a cold journey before you."

Jack knew better manners than to refuse the parting glass. "I wonder," he said, "will I be able to make out my way home?"

"What should ail you," said Coo, "when I'll show you the way?"

Out they went before the house, and Coomara took one of the cocked hats and put it upon Jack's head the wrong way. Then he lifted him up on his shoulder, so that he might launch him up into the water.

"Now," he said, giving him a heave, "you'll come up just in the same spot you came down in. And, Jack, mind and throw me back the hat."

He canted Jack off his shoulder, and up he shot like a bubble through the water, until he came to the very rock he had jumped off of, where he found a landing place. Then he threw the hat in the water, and it sank like a stone.

The sun was just going down in the beautiful sky of a calm summer's evening. A solitary star was dimly twinkling in the cloudless heaven, and the waves of the Atlantic flashed in a golden flood of light. So Jack, perceiving it was late, set off home. But when he got there, not a word did he say to Biddy of where he had spent his day.

THE STATE OF THE POOR SOULS cooped up in the lobster pots gave Jack a great deal of trouble, and determining how to release them cost him a great deal of thought. At first, he had a mind to speak to the priest about the matter. But what could the priest do, and what did Coo care for the priest? Besides, Coo was a good sort of an old fellow, and did not think he was doing any harm. It might also not be much to Jack's own credit if it were known that he used to go dine with merrows. On the whole, he thought his best plan would be to ask Coo to dinner, to make him drunk if he was able, and then to take the hat and go down and turn up the pots, releasing the souls. First of all, however, it was necessary to get Biddy out of the way, for Jack wished to keep the thing secret from her.

Accordingly, Jack grew mighty pious all of a sudden and said to Biddy that he thought it would be good for both their souls if she was to go to visit Saint John's Well. Biddy thought so too, and so she set off one fine morning at dawn, giving Jack a strict charge to keep an eye on the house. As soon as she was gone, away went Jack to the coast, to give the appointed signal to Coomara, which was throwing a big stone into the water. Jack threw, and up sprang Coomara.

"Good morning, Jack," said he. "What do you want with me?"

"Nothing at all, sir," replied Jack, "except for you to come and take a bit of dinner with me, if I might make so free as to ask you."

"It's quite agreeable, Jack, I assure you. What's your hour?"

"Any time that's most convenient to you, sir. Say one o'clock, that you may go home with the daylight."

"I'll be with you then," said Coo, "never fear me."

Jack went home, dressed a noble fish dinner, and got out plenty of his best foreign spirits, enough, for that matter, to make twenty men drunk. Just as the clock struck one, in came Coo with his cocked hat under his arm. Dinner was ready, and they sat down and ate and drank away manfully. Jack, thinking of the poor souls below in the pots, plied old Coo well with brandy and encouraged him to sing, hoping to put him under the table, but poor Jack forgot that he had not the sea over his own head to keep it cool. The brandy got into it and did his business for him, and Coo left his host as dumb as a haddock on a Good Friday.

Jack never woke until the next morning, and then he was in a sad way. "'Tis no use for me to try to make that old Coo drunk," said Jack. "How in this world can I help the poor souls out of the lobster pots?"

But after ruminating nearly the whole day, he was struck by an idea. "I have it," he said, slapping his knee. "I'll be sworn that Coo never saw a drop of poteen, as old as he is, and that's the thing to settle him! Is it not well that Biddy will not be home these two days yet? I can have another twist at him."

So Jack asked Coo again, and Coo laughed at him for having no better head, telling him he'd never live up to his grandfather.

"Well, try me again," said Jack, "and I'll drink you drunk and sober and drunk again."

"Anything in my power," said Coo, "to oblige you."

At this dinner, Jack took care to have his own liquor well-watered and to give the strongest brandy he had to Coo. At last he said, "Pray, sir, did you ever drink any poteen?"

"No," said Coo. "What's that, and where does it come from?"

"Oh, that's a secret," said Jack, "but it's the right stuff. Never believe me again if 'tis not fifty times as good as brandy or rum either. Biddy's brother just sent me a present of a little drop in exchange for some brandy, and as you're an old friend of the family, I kept it to treat you with."

"Well, let's see what sort of thing it is," said Coomara.

The poteen was the right sort. It was first-rate and had the real smack upon it. Coo was delighted. He drank and sang *Rum fum boodle boo* over and over again. And he laughed and danced until he fell on the floor fast asleep. Then Jack, who had taken good care to keep himself sober, snapped up the cocked hat, ran off to the rock, leaped in, and soon arrived at Coo's house.

All was as still as a churchyard at midnight. Not a merrow, old or young, was there. So in went Jack and turned up the pots, but he saw nothing emerge from them, only heard a sort of a little whistle or chirp as he raised each of them. At this he was surprised, until he recollected what the priests had often said, that nobody living could see the soul, no more than they could see the wind or the air. Having now done all that he could do for the sailors' souls, he set the pots as they were before and sent a blessing after the poor souls to speed them on their journey wherever they were going.

Jack now began to think of returning. He put the hat on the wrong way, but when he got outside he found the water so high over his head that he had no hope of ever getting up into it, now that old Coomara was not there to give him a lift. He walked about looking for a ladder, but not one could he find, nor was there a rock in sight. At last he saw a spot where the sea hung rather lower than anywhere else, so he resolved to try there. Just as he came to the spot, a big cod happened to put down his tail. Jack made a jump and caught hold of it, and the cod, all in amazement, gave a bounce and pulled Jack up. The minute the hat touched the water, Jack was whisked away and shot up like a cork, dragging the poor cod, which he forgot to let go of. He got to the rock in no time, and without a moment's delay hurried home, rejoicing in the good deed he had done.

But meanwhile, there was fine work at home, for Jack had hardly left the house on his soul-freeing expedition when Biddy came back from her soul-saving trip to the well. When she entered the house, she saw things lying higgledy-piggledy on the table before her.

"Here's a pretty job!" she said. "That blackguard husband of mine—what ill-luck I had ever to marry him!—has picked up some vagabond or other while I was praying for the good of his soul, and they've been drinking all the poteen that my own brother gave him and all the spirits that he was to have sold."

Then, hearing an outlandish kind of a grunt, she looked down and saw Coomara lying under the table.

"The blessed Virgin help me," she shouted, "if he has not made a real beast of himself! Well, well, I've often heard of a man making a beast of himself with drink! Oh, Jack, what will I do with you, or what will I do without you? How can any decent woman ever think of living with a beast?"

With such lamentations, Biddy rushed out of the house and was going she knew not where, when she heard the well-known voice of Jack singing a merry tune. She was glad enough to find him safe and sound and not turned into a thing that was like neither fish nor flesh. Then Jack was obliged to tell her all, and Biddy, though she had half a mind to be angry with him for not telling her before, admitted that he had done a great service to the poor souls.

Back they both went to the house, and Jack wakened up Coomara. Perceiving the old fellow to be rather dull, he bid him not to be cast down, for 'twas many a good man's case. It all came of his not being used to the poteen. Jack recommended to him, by way of cure, to swallow a hair of the dog that bit him. Coo, however, seemed to think he had had quite enough. He got up, quite out of sorts, and without having the manners to say one word in the way of civility, he sneaked off to cool himself by a jaunt through the salt water.

Coomara never missed the souls. He and Jack continued to be the best friends in the world, and no one, perhaps, ever equaled Jack for freeing souls from purgatory. For he contrived fifty excuses for getting into the house below the sea, unknown to the old fellow, and then turning up the pots and letting out the souls. It vexed him, to be sure, that he could never see them, but as he knew the thing to be impossible, he was obliged to be satisfied.

Their friendship continued for several years. However, one morning when Jack threw a stone in the water as usual, he got no answer. He flung another and another, but still there was no reply. He went away and returned the following morning, but it was to no avail. As he was without the hat, he could not go down to see what had become of old Coo, but his belief was that the old man, or the old fish, or whatever he was, had either died at last or had moved away from that part of the country.

3

—

QUESTS

THE BASIN of GOLD
and THE DIAMOND LANCE

Brittany

nce upon a time, near the town of Vannes, there lived an orphan boy named Peronnik. Brittany was in hard times, for the city of Nantes was besieged by the French, and the French soldiers had so devastated the surrounding country that there was nothing left but shrubs for the goats to nibble. The people were starving, and the soldiers of Brittany who had not died of wounds were dying of hunger. But Peronnik was a happy and resourceful lad. When he was hungry, he asked the farm women of the countryside for their broken bread. When he was thirsty, he drank at springs. And when he was sleepy, he sought out a haystack and curled himself within its shade.

One day, Peronnik came to a farmhouse built on the edge of a forest, and as he was well-nigh famished, he went to the door and asked for a crust of bread. The farmer's wife was scraping out the porridge pot with a flint, and she gave Peronnik the pot to finish. He sat down on the doorstep and, putting the saucepan between his knees, began to scrape away with a will.

"This is oatmeal fit for a king," he exclaimed, 'twixt ravenous mouthfuls.

The farmer's wife was delighted at the praise of her porridge. "Poor lone boy," she said, "there is not much left, but I will give you some homemade bread."

She brought the lad a small loaf fresh from the oven, and he bit into it like a wolf, declaring that it must have been kneaded by the baker of My Lord Bishop of Vannes. The peasant woman, bursting with pride to hear her bread so applauded, said it was much better with butter. And she brought Peronnik a pot of butter freshly churned. Peronnik spread it on the bread, declaring there was no butter like it in all the land of Brittany, and the dame was so delighted that she gave him a bit of last Sunday's bacon. The boy swallowed it as if it were spring water, for it had been many a long day since he had been so bounteously fed.

While Peronnik was enjoying himself thus, a knight came riding by and asked the farmwife the way to the Castle of Kerglas.

"Blessings on us! Can it be that you are going there?" asked the woman in astonishment.

"Yes," replied the knight, "and for that purpose I have come from a country so far away that I have been traveling day and night for many moons."

"And what do you seek at Kerglas?" the dame inquired.

"I am seeking the golden basin and the diamond lance," the stranger answered.

"Are they very valuable?" asked Peronnik, who had been listening with both ears.

"They are worth more than all the kings' crowns in the world," replied the knight. "For not only does the golden basin give you all the food you may desire, but if you drink from it you will be cured of any sickness. As for the diamond lance, it will destroy all that it strikes."

"And who has this basin of gold and this diamond lance?" asked Peronnik, amazed.

"They belong to a wizard named Rogéar," interrupted the farmwife, who had heard of the wizard before. "He is a giant, and lives in the Castle of Kerglas. You may often see him ride near the edge of the forest. He rides a black mare who is followed by her foal. No one dares attack the wizard, for he carries the magic lance."

"Yet I am told he does not bear it in the castle," said the knight. "Rogéar locks his lance and his basin in a dark keep beneath the ground, which no key can open. I plan to attack the wizard and win his magic treasures."

"You will never succeed, good Sir Knight," said the farmwife. "More than a hundred noblemen have tried this adventure, but not one has ever returned."

"I know that full well, worthy dame," answered the knight, "but I have had instructions from the hermit of Polavet."

"What did the hermit tell you?" asked Peronnik eagerly.

"He warned me that I must pass through a wood where magic spells await me, and where I may lose my way," the knight replied. "If I succeed in passing through the wood, I shall meet an elf armed with a fiery dart that turns all it touches to ashes. This elf is guarding an apple tree from which I must pick an apple."

"And after that?" queried Peronnik.

"I must find the flower that laughs," the knight continued. "It is guarded by a lion whose mane is formed of vipers. But I must pluck the flower. Then I shall have to cross the lake of twelve dragons and fight the six-eyed man. He is armed with an iron ball, which always hits its mark and then returns to its master."

"Is that all?" Peronnik asked.

"No," answered the knight, "for finally I must go through the Valley of Delights, where I shall see everything that can tempt and hold me back. Then when I pass the valley, I shall come to a river with a single ford. There shall I find a lady draped in black. I must carry her across the river, and she will tell me what I must do next to gain my quest."

The farmwife tried to persuade the knight not to undertake the venture. She felt assured no man could successfully undergo all these dire ordeals.

"This is not a matter that a woman can judge," announced the strange knight haughtily, and after the entrance to the forest had been pointed out to him, he spurred his horse and disappeared among the trees. The woman sighed, declaring that there would soon be another soul before the throne of judgment.

Peronnik was about to go upon his way when the farmer arrived from the fields. He was in need of a cowherd, and he had no sooner seen Peronnik than he decided to hire him. Peronnik was delighted to enter the farmer's service because of the good food he knew the farmer's wife would give him. So out to the field on the edge of the forest he went, to watch the cows and to bring them home at sunset.

One day shortly after this, as he was running to and fro among the cows, Peronnik heard the sound of horses' hooves, and looking toward the forest, he saw the giant Rogéar riding his black mare and followed by her foal. On a cord around the giant's neck hung the golden basin, and in his hand he bore the diamond lance. Peronnik, frightened, hid behind a bush until the giant had passed by and disappeared among the trees.

Several times after this, the wizard Rogéar rode past Peronnik, until at length the boy grew quite used to seeing him and no longer ran to hide. Instead, Peronnik fell to thinking how much he himself wished to follow the adventure of which the knight had told. "And what a glorious thing it would be," he mused, "to get possession of the golden basin and the diamond lance!"

One afternoon when Peronnik was alone in the meadow watching the cattle, he saw a man with a flowing beard standing at the edge of the forest. Peronnik wondered whether he were a stranger come, like the knight, to seek his fortune. Approaching the bearded figure, he asked him if he were looking for the road to the Castle of Kerglas.

"No, I am not looking for it," answered the stranger, "for I already know it."

"You have been to Kerglas and the giant did not kill you!" exclaimed Peronnik.

"Rogéar has nothing to fear from me," the white-bearded man replied. "I am the sorcerer Bryak, Rogéar's elder brother. When I wish to see him, I come here, and, as I cannot go through the enchanted wood without being lost in spite of my magic power, I call the black colt to show me the way."

As he spoke, he stooped over and drew three circles in the dust, muttering magic words, and then cried aloud:

"Foal, free of foot
Foal, free of tongue,
Foal, here am I.
Come to me, O come,
Free of foot and tongue,
Foal, here wait I."

The little horse appeared at once. Bryak put a bridle on him, swung up on his back, and disappeared into the forest.

Peronnik said nothing of this to anyone, but now he understood that the first thing necessary to get to the Castle of Kerglas was to ride the colt, who knew the way. The boy did not know how to draw magic circles, nor how to say the magic words, but he did remember the verse to call the colt. And he had thought long and hard about the tasks that lay before him: to gather the apple, pluck the flower that laughs, cross the lake of dragons, escape from the six-eyed man, and pass through the Valley of Delights.

So Peronnik made a bridle of flax, a snare to catch snipe which he dipped in holy water, and a linen bag which he filled with glue and larks' feathers. Then he took his rosary, a wooden whistle, and a bit of bread rubbed with rancid bacon. With these things, Peronnik was ready to begin the adventure.

The next morning, he took the bread the farmer's wife had given him, and crumbled it along the path that the giant Rogéar would be sure to follow. In a short time, Rogéar appeared out of the woods and crossed the meadow just as he had done before. But this time the colt, smelling the bread, sniffed the ground and stopped to eat the crumbs, and thus was soon left alone as the giant on horseback passed quickly on among the trees.

Then Peronnik sang in his clear voice:

"Foal, free of foot
Foal, free of tongue,
Foal, here am I.
Come to me, O come,
Free of foot and tongue,
Foal, here wait I."

The foal stopped, turned, and quickly came to Peronnik, who gently bridled him. The lad then jumped up on his back and gave the colt his head, for he was sure the colt knew the way to Kerglas. And indeed, without the slightest hesitation, the colt took one of the wildest paths into the forest and trotted quickly into its gloomy depths.

The ride was terrible to Peronnik, and he trembled with fear, for the forest was enchanted and spells were cast to terrify him. The trees appeared to be in flames or loomed appallingly like specters of some nether world, the streams became enraged torrents, and overhanging rocks seemed about to topple. Peronnik pulled his cap over his eyes so he could not see what dread shapes surrounded him, and the colt bounded ever forward.

At last they came out of the forest to a plain where the spells were ended. Peronnik now dared to look about him. It was a desolate spot, and here and there were skeletons of nobles who had come to seek the Castle of Kerglas. Peronnik, shuddering, passed quickly onward and came at length to a meadow shaded by a mighty apple tree that groaned beneath its load of fruit. Near the tree stood an elf, and in his hand was the fiery dart that turned all that it touched to ashes.

When the elf saw Peronnik, he uttered a loud cry and instantly raised the dart.

But Peronnik, without appearing at all to look surprised, took his cap in his hand and said politely, "Do not bother about me, little prince, I am going through the meadow only to reach Kerglas."

"And who are you?" demanded the elf, lowering his arm.

"I am Peronnik, you know," answered the boy.

"I know nothing of the kind," retorted the elf.

"I pray you to not let me waste my time," said Peronnik. "I have the wizard's colt, and I must take it on to Kerglas."

The elf, seeing that he indeed did have the colt, was about to let him pass when he noticed the snare Peronnik was carrying.

"What is that for?" he asked.

"That is to catch birds," Peronnik replied. "Nothing that flies can escape its meshes."

"I should like to be assured of that," said the elf. "My apple tree is plundered by the blackbirds. Get your snare ready, and if you catch a blackbird, I will agree to let you pass."

Peronnik accepted the proposal. He tied the colt to a branch, then went to the trunk of the tree, fixed one end of the snare to it, and asked the elf to hold the other end while he prepared the pegs. The elf did so. Then Peronnik deftly tightened the slipknot, and in a trice, the elf found himself captured in the snare.

The elf uttered a howl of rage and fought to free himself, but the cord, which had been dipped in holy water, held him tightly. Peronnik picked an apple from the tree, mounted once more upon the back of the foal, and rode off while the elf still raged within the snare.

Peronnik soon left the plain behind him and came to a lovely glade with sweet shrubs and plants of every delicious fragrance. In the midst of all nodded the mysterious laughing flower. But a lion was guarding this glade. He had a mane of vipers, and his growl resounded like the rumblings of thunder.

Peronnik took off his cap to the lion, wished him good luck, and then asked if this were the right road to Kerglas.

"And what business have you at Kerglas?" roared the lion, fire flashing from his eyes.

"I am returning the wizard's colt, do you not see?" Peronnik asked in return.

Well, yes, the lion did see it. "But before I let you pass, reveal the contents of your bag," commanded the mighty beast, approaching Peronnik and sniffing the sack which held the feathers and the glue.

"I shall be glad to," said the boy, "but beware, for what is in it might fly out."

"Birds! Open it a little then, and let me look in," growled the beast, who by now had become very curious indeed.

That was just what Peronnik wanted, so he held out the bag half-opened, and the lion plunged in his head. Of course the feathers and the glue stuck to him. Peronnik quickly pulled the string and fastened it tightly around the lion's neck. Then he rushed toward the laughing flower, plucked it, and rode off as swiftly as the colt could carry him.

Riding thus, it did not take long to reach the lake of the twelve dragons. Across this the lad and the colt had to swim, and hardly had they touched the water than the dragons came crowding to devour them. This time Peronnik did not trouble to take off his cap. He began at once to throw the beads of his rosary to the dragons, who snapped at them as if they had been cherries. As each dragon swallowed a bead, he rolled over on his back and died. Thus Peronnik and the colt swam safely to the far side of the lake.

But Peronnik had yet to enter the valley watched over by the six-eyed man, and before long he beheld this sinister figure in the narrow entrance to the valley. He was chained to a rock by one foot, and he had in his hand the iron ball which always hit that at which it was thrown and then returned to its master. His six eyes each took their turns watching while the others slept, so that it was impossible to pass into the valley without the man seeing. And at this moment, all six eyes were open.

Peronnik knew that if the six-eyed man saw him, he would hurl the iron ball and it would crush him. So he dodged among the woods and in this way managed to get quite close to the man, who had just sat down to rest and had closed two of his eyes.

Encouraged by this, Peronnik began to sing a lullaby in his soft and musical voice, and the man shut his third and fourth eyes. Peronnik sang on, and the man slowly closed his fifth eye. The lad then began to chant the vespers, and before he had finished, the six-eyed man was fast asleep. The lad now took the colt by the bridle and led him noiselessly over the grass-grown road. He passed the six-eyed man without a sound and entered at length the Valley of Delights.

This valley resembled a lush garden with blossoms, fruit trees, and sparkling fountains. The fountains played wine instead of water, the flowers sang, and the trees reached down their branches and offered their bounteous harvest. Peronnik saw tables spread as for a king. He smelled the delicious odor of fresh cakes. Servants waited for his commands. Beautiful maidens danced upon the flower-spangled lawns. They called to him by name and invited him to join the revelry.

Peronnik had all but alighted from the colt, and at once all would have been over for him, when suddenly the memory of the golden basin and the diamond lance bade him pause. He quickly pulled out his wooden whistle and began to pipe upon it so as not to hear the sweet voices of the maidens. He ate his bread and rancid bacon so that he no longer smelled the enticing food upon the tables. And he fixed his eyes on the colt's ears and so could not see the lovely dancers.

In this way he proceeded through the valley without any mishap and at last in the distance beheld the Castle of Kerglas. But he was cut off from it by the river with one ford. The colt knew the ford well and, going directly to it, strode out into the water. Then Peronnik looked about him to find the lady who was to take him to the castle, and there she was seated on a rock. She was dressed in black satin and her face was as dark as the shadows of night.

Peronnik pulled in the colt and, taking off his cap, bowed to the lady.

"I have been waiting for you," she said.

"Will you tell me what to do next?" Peronnik asked.

"Yes," replied the dark lady, "if you will take me across the river."

Peronnik helped her to mount behind him and then continued to ford the river.

"Listen," said the lady. "The apple tree which was guarded by the elf is a magic tree, and if you can persuade the giant Rogéar to eat the apple which you have brought, you may win the golden basin and the diamond lance."

"I shall try," said Peronnik. "And if I succeed, how can I obtain the basin and the lance? Are they not hidden in a dark underground chamber which no key can open?"

"The flower that laughs," she answered, "opens every door and lights the darkest places."

Talking thus, they reached the farthest bank. There Peronnik parted with the lady and, dismounting from the colt, walked toward the castle.

Before the entrance gate sat the giant, smoking a pipe of pure gold. When he saw Peronnik alighting from the foal, he shouted in a voice like thunder, "By all the magic powers! That is my colt the young scapegrace is riding!"

"Yes, it is, greatest of all magicians," said Peronnik, bowing and taking off his cap.

"And how did you lay hands on it?" the giant roared.

"I repeated what I learned from the sorcerer Bryak, your brother," returned Peronnik.

"Foal, free of foot
Foal, free of tongue,
Foal, here am I.
Come to me, O come,
Free of foot and tongue,
Foal, here wait I."

"Humph! And what do you want?" demanded the giant.

"I have brought you a rare gift from your brother Bryak," Peronnik said. "This magic apple, which will make glad your heart."

"So be it, then. Give me the apple," said the giant.

Peronnik obeyed, and Rogéar took the apple. But no sooner had he bitten into it, than he turned suddenly into a dwarf so small that he did not reach the top of Peronnik's shoe. Leaving him raging and running about in circles, the lad then entered the castle holding the laughing flower. He passed through fifty rooms and one and came at last to a silver door. The door was locked with a ponderous lock, but, yielding to the laughing flower, it swung open. Peronnik, still holding the flower before him, entered and beheld the golden basin and the diamond lance.

Hardly had he seized them than the earth began to quake. Thunder rolled and lightning flared, and suddenly the castle vanished and Peronnik found himself once more in the field among the cows. But in his hands he clasped the golden basin and the diamond lance.

Carrying these treasures, Peronnik set out at once for the court of the king of Brittany. When he came to the besieged city of Nantes, a herald was proclaiming that the king would adopt as his heir the man who would deliver the city from the French.

When Peronnik heard this he said to the herald, "Read your proclamation no more and take me to the king, for I am he whom he seeks."

When Peronnik came before the king, he showed him the golden basin and the diamond lance. The king was delighted and promised to make Peronnik his heir if the lad could free Nantes from the besiegers.

And the king fulfilled his word. For with the diamond lance Peronnik quickly swept Brittany of all its enemies, and with the golden basin he restored the wounded Breton soldiers. Peronnik became rich and had many children, to each of whom he gave a kingdom when he inherited the throne. But some say that the wizard Rogéar succeeded in winning back the golden basin and the diamond lance and that no one now can ever find them, no matter where they seek.

THE BROWNIE
of FERN GLEN

—

Scotland

here was once a farmhouse called Fern Glen. It was named for the glen which it stood on the edge of, and which anyone who wanted to visit the farm had to travel through. But this glen was believed to be the abode of a brownie. This fairy never appeared to anyone in the daytime, but was sometimes glimpsed at night, stealing about like an ungainly shadow from tree to tree.

Like all brownies who are properly treated and let alone, he would do any kind of work around the farm in return for a bowl of milk for his supper. The farmer often said that he did not know what he would do without the brownie, for if there was any work to be finished in a hurry at the farm—corn to thrash or winnow, turnips to cut, clothes to wash, or a garden to be weeded—all that the farmer and his wife had to do was to leave the door of the barn or the turnip shed or the milk house open when they went to bed and put down a bowl of new milk on the doorstep. And when they woke the next morning, the bowl would be empty and the job finished better than if it had been done by mortal hands.

In spite of all this, however, everyone about the farm was afraid of the brownie and would rather go a couple of miles round about in the dark than pass through the glen and run the risk of catching a glimpse of him.

Only one person on the farm didn't fear the brownie, and that was the farmer's wife. She was good and gentle and wasn't afraid of anything at all. So when the brownie's supper had to be left outside, she always filled his bowl with the richest milk and added a good spoonful of cream to it, for, she said, "He works so hard for us and asks no wages, and he well deserves the very best meal that we can give him."

One night this gentle lady was taken very ill, and everyone was afraid she was going to die. The farmer was greatly distressed, and so were the servants and farmhands, for she had been such a good mistress to all of them that they loved her as if she had been their mother. But they were all young, and none of them knew very much about illness, so everyone agreed that it would be better to send off for an old woman who lived about seven miles away on the other side of the river, and who was known to be a very skillful nurse.

But who was to go? That was the question. For it was black midnight, and the way to the old woman's house lay straight through the glen. Whoever traveled that road at night ran the risk of meeting the dreaded brownie.

The farmer would have gone only too willingly, but he dared not leave his wife alone. So the servants stood in groups about the kitchen, each one telling the other that he or she ought to go, yet none of them offering to go themselves. Little did they know that the cause of all their terror was standing only a yard or two away, listening with an anxious face from behind the kitchen door.

The brownie was a queer, misshapen, wee man, with a long beard, red-rimmed eyes, broad, flat feet, and enormous long arms that touched the ground even when he stood upright. He had come up from his hiding place in the glen as he did every night, to see if there was any work for him to do, and to look for his bowl of milk. But he had seen from the open door and lit-up windows that there was something wrong inside the farm-house, which at that hour was wont to be dark and still. So he had crept in through the back door to try and find out what the matter was.

When he gathered from the servants' talk that the farmer's wife, who had been so kind to him, was taken ill, his heart sank within him. And when he heard that the silly servants were so taken up with their own fears that they dared not set out to fetch a nurse for her, he became angry.

"Fools, idiots, dolts!" he muttered to himself, stamping his queer, misshapen feet on the floor. "They speak as if I were ready to take a bite out of them as soon as ever I met them. If they only knew the bother it gives me to keep out of their road! But if they go on like this, the bonnie lady will surely die. So it seems that I must go and fetch help myself."

So saying, he reached up his long arm and took down the farmer's dark cloak from a peg on the wall. Quickly and quietly, he threw it over his head and shoulders to hide his ungainly form and hurried away to the stable. The horses and other animals were not afraid of the brownie, for they often saw him in the night working away at whatever task had been left for him. So they didn't stir as the brownie saddled and bridled the fastest horse, led him to the door of the stable, and scrambled up on his back.

Then the brownie whispered to the horse, "If ever you traveled fleetly, travel fleetly now." And it was as if the creature understood him, for it gave a little whinny and pricked up its ears and then darted out into the darkness like an arrow from the bow.

Never before had the road to the old woman's cottage been ridden so fast before. But when the brownie drew rein outside the cottage, the old woman was in bed, fast asleep. He hurried up to the door and rapped sharply, and the woman, who was accustomed to being roused in the night on account of her skill in healing, rose and peered through the peephole to see who was at the door.

The brownie pulled his cloak close about his face and told her his errand in his low, gravelly voice. "The mistress of Fern Glen is ill," he said, "and there is no one to nurse her but a bunch of empty-headed servants. Will you come with me, and quickly, to save her life?"

"But how am I to get there? Have they sent a cart for me?" asked the old woman anxiously, for she was familiar with the way to the farm and was nervous of meeting the brownie in the glen.

"No, they have sent no cart," replied the brownie shortly. "So you must just climb up behind me on the saddle and hang on tight to my waist, and I promise to bring you to Fern Glen farm safe and sound."

So the old woman made haste to dress herself and gather her nurse's bag. Then she unlocked her door and clambered up onto the horse's back behind the dark-cloaked stranger. Not a word was spoken until they approached the dreaded glen. Then the old woman felt her courage giving way. "Do you think that there will be any chance of meeting the brownie?" she asked tremulously. "I would fain not run the risk, for folk say that he is an unchancy creature."

Her companion gave a curious laugh. "Keep up your heart, and don't talk nonsense," he said, "for I promise you'll see naught uglier this night than the man whom you ride behind."

"Oh, then, I'm fine and safe," replied the old woman, with a sigh of relief. "For although I haven't seen your face, I warrant that you are a good man, from the care you have shown for your mistress at the farm."

She lapsed into silence again until they had passed through the glen and the good horse had turned into the farmyard. Then the brownie slid to the ground, turned round, and lifted the old woman carefully down with his long, strong arms. But as he did so, the cloak slipped off him, revealing his fearsome face and misshapen limbs.

The old woman gasped. "What kind of man are you?" she asked, peering into his face in the grey morning light, which was just dawning. "What makes your eyes so big? And what have you done to your feet? They are more like a frog's feet than a man's."

The brownie drew back. He dreaded to be seen by mortals, and so he hurried to pull the cloak back up over his head. "Please," he said, "waste no time in talking. The lady inside is ill and needs your help." And he started to hurry away, back toward the glen.

"Very well," the old woman called after him, "but I think I have guessed who you are. And although you won't come inside and take the credit for your deeds tonight, I'm sure the farmer and his wife would be only too glad to thank you."

The brownie paused at the edge of the farmyard, and then he turned back to say, "I don't need any more thanks for my work than a good bowl of milk, but it grieves me to be thought ill of, and I wish they wouldn't avoid the glen on my account. Tell them that from the brownie of Fern Glen," he said, and then he disappeared into the trees.

And the old woman did just that. After she had tended to the farmer's wife and made sure she was to get well again, she sat the rest of them down and recounted her adventure. So forever after, although they never saw the brownie any more than they had before, the people of Fern Glen were no longer afraid of him or of passing through the glen. And when they put out a bowl of milk on the doorstep, they always made sure to fill it with the richest milk and to add a good spoonful of cream, too.

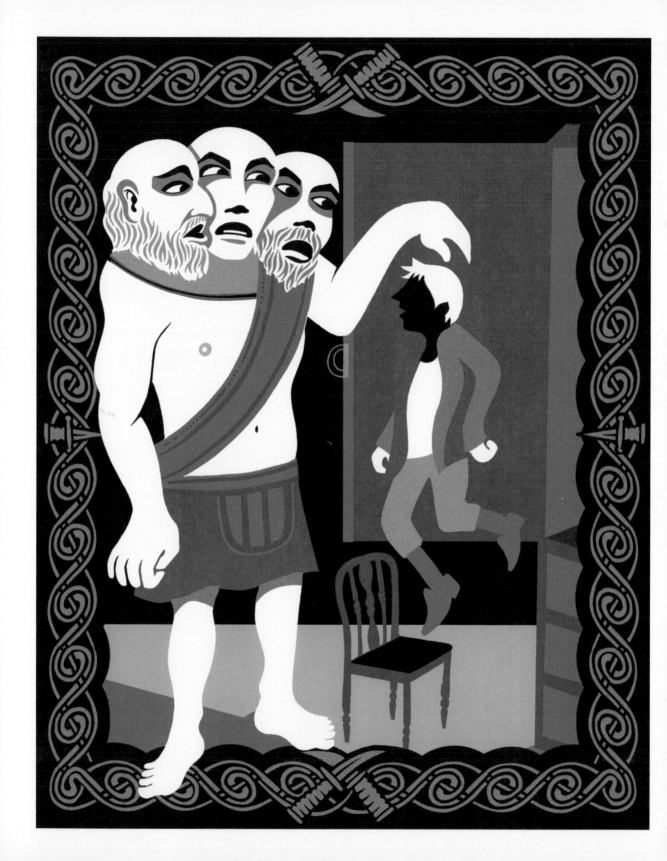

THE RED-ETIN

Scotland

here once was a widow with three sons. They lived on a little piece of land where they grazed a cow and a few sheep, and in this way they made their living. But at last the time arrived when the eldest son must leave home and go out into the world to seek his fortune. The night before he went away, his mother told him to take a can down to the well and bring back some water, and she would bake a cake that he could carry with him.

"But remember," she added, "the size of the cake will depend on the quantity of water that you bring back. If you bring much, then will it be large, and if you bring little, then will it be small. Big or little, it is all that I have to give you."

The lad took the can and went off to the well, filled it with water, and came home again. But he never noticed that the can had a hole in it and the water was running out, so that, by the time he arrived at home, there was very little water left. So his mother could only bake him a very little cake.

Small as it was, she asked him, as she gave it to him, to choose one of two things: either to take the whole cake or to take half the cake and her blessing. The lad looked at the cake and hesitated. It would have been pleasant to have left home with his mother's blessing upon him, but he had far to go, and the cake was little. The half of it would be a mere mouthful, and he did not know when he would get any more food. So at last he made up his mind to take the whole of it without the blessing.

Then he took his younger brother, the middle son, aside and gave him his hunting knife, saying, "Keep this with you, and look at it every morning. For as long as the blade remains clear and bright, you will know that all is well with me, but should it grow dim and rusty, then you will know that some evil has befallen me."

After this he embraced his family and set out on his travels. He journeyed all that day and all the next, and on the afternoon of the third day, he came to where an old shepherd was struggling to herd a large flock of sheep across a field.

"I will ask the old man whose sheep they are," he said to himself, "for maybe his master might engage me as a shepherd." So he went up to the old man and asked him to whom the sheep belonged. And this was all the answer he got:

"The Red-Etin of Ireland
Ance lived in Ballygan,
And stole King Malcolm's daughter,
The king of fair Scotland.
He beats her, he binds her,
He lays her on a band
And every day he dings her
With a bright silver wand.
Like Julian the Roman,
He's one that fears no man.
It's said there's ane predestinate
To be his mortal foe,
But that man is yet unborn,
And lang may it be so."

"That does not tell me much, but somehow I do not fancy this Red-Etin for a master," thought the youth, and he went on his way.

He had not gone very far, however, when he saw another old man, with snow-white hair, herding a flock of swine. As he wondered to whom the swine belonged, and if there was any chance of him getting a situation as a swineherd, he went up to the man and asked who was the owner of the animals.

He got the same answer from the swineherd that he had got from the shepherd:

"The Red-Etin of Ireland
Ance lived in Ballygan,
And stole King Malcolm's daughter,
The king of fair Scotland.
He beats her, he binds her,
He lays her on a band
And every day he dings her
With a bright silver wand.
Like Julian the Roman,
He's one that fears no man.
It's said there's ane predestinate
To be his mortal foe,
But that man is yet unborn,
And lang may it be so."

"Plague on this old Red-Etin. I wonder when I will get out of his domains," muttered the youth, and he journeyed still farther.

Presently he came to a very, very old man—so old, indeed, that he was quite bent with age—who was herding a flock of goats. Once more the traveler asked to whom the animals belonged, and once more he got the same answer.

So the young man went on his way, but he had not gone very far before he met a herd of very dreadful creatures, unlike anything that he had ever dreamed of in all his life. Each of them had three heads, and on each of its three heads it had four horns. When the youth saw them, he was so frightened that he turned and ran away from them as fast as he could.

Up hill and down dale he ran, until he was well-nigh exhausted, and was sure the horrible creatures would catch up with him. But just when he was beginning to feel that his legs would not carry him any farther, he saw a great castle in front of him, the door of which was standing wide open. He went straight in and slammed the door behind him.

When he had recovered his breath, he began to wander through the magnificent halls, which appeared to be quite deserted. At last he reached the kitchen, where an old woman was sitting by the fire. He asked her if he might have a night's lodging, as he had had a long and weary journey, and would be glad of somewhere to rest.

"You can rest here, and you're welcome to," said the old dame, "but for your own sake I warn you that this is an ill house to bide in. For it is the castle of the Red-Etin, who is a fierce and terrible monster with three heads, and he spares neither man nor woman if he can get hold of them."

Tired as he was, the young man would have made an effort to escape from such a dangerous abode had he not remembered the strange and awful beasts from which he had just been fleeing. He was afraid that if he set out again in the growing dark, he might chance to walk right into their midst. So he begged the old woman to hide him in some dark corner, and not to tell the Red-Etin that he was in the castle.

"For," he thought, "if I can only get shelter until the morning, I will then be able to avoid these terrible creatures and go on my way in peace."

So the old dame hid him in a big cupboard under the back stairs, and, as there was plenty of room in it, he settled down quite comfortably for the night.

But just as he was going off to sleep, he heard an awful roaring and trampling overhead. The Red-Etin had come home, and it was plain that he was searching for something. The terrified youth soon found out what that was, for the horrible monster came into the kitchen, crying out in a voice like thunder:

"Seek but, and seek ben,
I smell the smell of an earthly man!
Be he living, or be he dead,
His heart this night I shall eat with my bread."

It was not very long before he discovered the poor young man's hiding place and pulled him roughly out of it. Of course, the lad begged that his life might be spared, but the monster only laughed at him.

"It will be spared if you can answer three questions," he said. "If not, it is forfeited."

The first of these three questions was, "Which was first inhabited, Ireland or Scotland?"

The second was, "Which were created first, men or beasts?"

And the third was, "How old was the world when Adam was made?"

The lad was not skilled in such matters, having had but little book learning, and he could not answer the questions. So the monster struck him on the head with a queer little hammer which he carried, and turned him into a piece of stone.

Now, every morning since he had left home, his younger brother had done as he promised and had carefully examined the hunting knife. On the first two mornings it was bright and clear, but on the third morning he was very much distressed to find that it was suddenly dull and rusty. He looked at it for a few moments in great dismay. Then he ran straight to his mother, and held it out to her.

"By this token I know that some mischief has befallen my brother," he said, "so I must set out at once to see what evil has come upon him."

"First you must go to the well and fetch me some water," said his mother, "that I may bake you a cake to carry with you, as I baked a cake for your brother. And I will say to you what I said to him, that the cake will be large or small according as you bring much or little water back with you."

So the lad took the can, as his brother had done, and went off to the well. And it seemed as if some evil spirit directed him to follow his brother's example in all things, for the can leaked and he brought home little water, and he chose the whole cake instead of half and his mother's blessing. He gave the hunting knife to his brother, the youngest, to watch over in case some evil should befall him. Then he set out and met the shepherd, the swineherd, and the goatherd. He asked each one who owned their herds, and they all gave the same answer to him which they had given to his brother. He also encountered the same fierce beasts, ran from them in terror, and took shelter from them in the castle. The old woman hid him, and the Red-Etin found him, and, because he could not answer the three questions, he, too, was turned into a pillar of stone.

The next morning when the youngest son looked at the knife, it was rusted again, and he knew that both his brothers were now in need of his help. He determined to set out to find them, and from the very first moment that he had made up his mind to do so, things went differently with him than they had with his brothers.

When his mother sent him to fetch water from the well so that she might bake a cake for him, a raven flying above his head croaked out that his can was leaking, and the youth, wishing to please his mother by bringing her a good supply of water, patched up the hole with clay, and so came home with the can quite full.

Then, when his mother had baked a large cake for him, and gave him his choice between the whole cake or half of it and her blessing, he chose the latter.

"For," he said, throwing his arms round her neck, "I may light on other cakes to eat, but I will never light on another blessing such as yours."

Then he started on his journey, and after he had walked for many miles, he came to the old shepherd herding his sheep. Instead of asking straight-away to whom the sheep belonged, as his brothers had done, the youth offered first to help the old shepherd, and together they drove the sheep easily across the field. When they finished the work, the shepherd said he had nothing to offer the youth as payment except a bit of knowledge, which was that neither Ireland nor Scotland was inhabited first, for they were first peopled at the very same time.

The youth did not know what to make of this, but he thanked the shepherd and asked him, before he went on his way, to whom the sheep belonged.

And this time the old man answered:

"The Red-Etin of Ireland
Ance lived in Ballygan,
And stole King Malcolm's daughter,
The king of fair Scotland.
He beats her, he binds her,
He lays her on a band
And every day he dings her
With a bright silver wand.
Like Julian the Roman,
He's one that fears no man.
But now I fear his end is near,
And destiny at hand;
And you're to be, I plainly see,
The heir to all his land."

The young man traveled on quite puzzled, until he came to the swine-herd. He offered to help the man with the herd, just as he had done before. When the work was done, the swineherd also offered him a bit of knowledge in recompense, which was that neither men nor beasts were created before the other, but they were created at the very same time. And when the lad asked him who owned the swine, the old man repeated the same words as the shepherd.

Again the youth went on his way, and when he came to the goatherd, it all went in the same way. The goatherd offered him the knowledge that when Adam was born, the earth was so young it did not have an age, and then he repeated the verse that the shepherd and the swineherd had said before him. But to this, the ancient goatherd added some advice.

"Beware, stranger," he said, "of the next herd of beasts that you meet. Sheep, swine, and goats will harm nobody, but the creatures you shall now encounter are of a sort that you have never met before, and they are not harmless."

Sure enough, the lad met the drove of monstrous beasts, but he was not afraid. He faced the creatures and fended them off with the hunting knife, and as soon as they saw that he was not afraid of them, they became docile and wandered away. He followed the creatures boldly, and they led him straight to the castle of the Red-Etin.

The halls were deserted as before, but in the kitchen he met the old woman, who warned him gravely not to linger there.

"Your two brothers came here before you," she said, "and they are now turned into two pillars of stone. What advantage is it to you to lose your life also?"

But the young man was determined to stay and face the monster, so, much against her will, the old woman let him in and hid him where she had hid his brothers.

It was not long before the Red-Etin arrived, and as on former occasions, he came into the kitchen in a furious rage, crying:

"Seek but, and seek ben,
I smell the smell of an earthly man!

Be he living, or be he dead,

His heart this night I shall eat with my bread."

Then he peered into the young man's hiding place and called to him to come out. He said he would spare the lad's life if he could answer three questions.

"The first question," he said, "is this: Which was first inhabited, Ireland or Scotland?"

"Neither," said the youth, "for they were peopled at the very same time."

The monster frowned, but he went on to ask the second question: "Which were created first, men or beasts?"

"Neither," said the youth, "for they were created at the very same time."

Growing angry, the monster cried, "How old was the world when Adam was made?"

"It was so young that it had no age," said the youth.

Then the Red-Etin's heart sank within him, for he knew that someone had betrayed him and that his power was gone.

And gone in very truth it was. For when the youth took his knife and attacked the monster, he had no strength to resist, and before he knew where he was, all three of his heads were cut off. And that was the end of the Red-Etin.

As soon as he had made sure that his enemy was really dead, and, on a whim, had taken the little hammer from his belt, the young man asked the old woman if what the shepherd, the swineherd, and the goatherd had told him were true, and if King Malcolm's daughter were really a prisoner in the castle.

The old woman nodded. "Even with the monster lying dead at my feet, I am almost afraid to speak of it," she said. "But come with me, my gallant gentleman, and you will see what misery the Red-Etin has caused."

She took a large key and led him up a long flight of stairs and down a passage which ended in a locked door. She opened it with the key and said, "You have naught to fear now, Madam. The Predestinated Deliverer has come, and the Red-Etin is dead."

With a cry of joy, a young lady came out of the room, more beautiful and more stately than any the lad had ever seen. When the youth stepped forward and bowed down before her, she spoke so sweetly to him, greeted him so gladly, and called him her deliverer in such a low, clear voice that his heart was taken captive at once.

But he did not forget his brothers. He asked the old woman where they were, and she took him to the other end of the passage, where there was another locked door. When she unlocked it, he stepped through into a room so dark that one could scarcely see in it, and so low that one could scarcely stand upright. In this dismal chamber stood two blocks of stone.

"One can unlock doors, young master," said the old woman, shaking her head forebodingly, "but 'tis hard work to try to turn cold stone back to flesh and blood."

"Nevertheless, I will do it," said the youth. He lifted the little hammer which he had taken from the monster's belt, and tapped each of the stone pillars lightly on the top.

Instantly, the hard stone seemed to soften and melt away, and his two brothers started into life and form again. Their gratitude to their brother, who had risked so much to save them, knew no bounds, while for his part, he was delighted to think that his efforts had been successful.

The next thing to do was to convey the princess back to the King's Court, and this they did the very next day. King Malcolm was so overjoyed to see his dearly loved daughter safe and sound when he had given her up for dead, and so grateful to her deliverer, that he said that the youth should become his son-in-law and marry the princess. And so it came to pass. As for the other two young men, they married noblemen's daughters, and their old mother came to live at court, too, and everyone was as happy as they could possibly be.

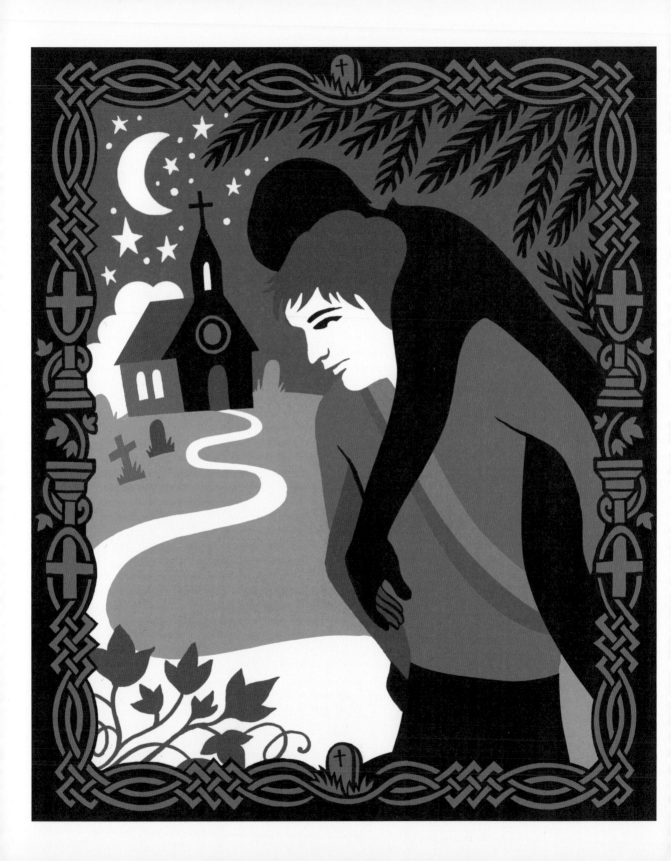

TEIG O'KANE
and THE CORPSE

—

Ireland

here was once a lad in County Leitrim called Teig O'Kane. His father, a rich farmer, had no other children, and he loved Teig so much that he allowed him to do everything just as it pleased himself. Accordingly, when the boy grew up, he liked sport better than work. He was very extravagant and seldom to be found at home—but if there was a fair or a race or any kind of gathering within ten miles of him, you were dead certain to find him there. It's many the kiss he got and he gave, for he was very handsome, and there wasn't a girl in the country who, when he fastened his two eyes on her, would not fall in love with him.

At last Teig became very wild and unruly. He wasn't to be seen day nor night in his father's house, but was always rambling from place to place and from house to house, gambling and card-playing and drinking. The old people shook their heads and said, "It's easy to see what will happen to the land when the old man dies; his son will run through it in a year."

Despite all this, Teig's father never minded his bad habits and never punished him. But then one day, the old man was told that his son had ruined the character of a girl called Mary, and he was greatly angry.

He called Teig to him and said to him, quietly and sensibly, "Son, you know I loved you greatly up to this. I never stopped you from doing whatever you chose, I gave you plenty of money, and I always hoped to leave you the house and land and all I had after myself would be gone. But I heard a story of you today that has disgusted me with you. I cannot tell you the grief that I felt when I heard such a thing of you, and I tell you now plainly that unless you marry that girl, I'll leave house and land and everything to my brother's son. I could never leave it to anyone who would make so bad a use of it as you do yourself, deceiving women and coaxing girls. Settle with yourself now whether you'll marry that girl and get my land as a fortune with her, or refuse to marry her and give up all that was coming to you. And tell me in the morning which of the two things you have chosen." And with that, he left, before Teig could make a reply.

"Och!" Teig called after him. "Father, you wouldn't say that to me, and I such a good son. Who told you I wouldn't marry the girl?"

But his father was gone, and the lad knew well enough that he would keep his word, too. For as quiet and as kind as the father was, he never went back on a word that he had once said.

The boy did not know rightly what to do. He was in fact in love with Mary, and he hoped to marry her sometime or other, but he would much rather have remained another while as he was, drinking, sporting, and playing cards. And on top of that, he was angry that his father should order him to marry, and should threaten him if he did not do it.

"Isn't my father a great fool?" he said to himself. "I was ready enough, and only too anxious, to marry Mary; and now since he threatened me—faith, I've a great mind to let it go another while."

He walked out into the night at last to cool his heated blood. He lit a pipe, and, as the night was fine, he walked and walked along the road until the quick pace made him begin to forget his trouble. The night was bright and the moon half full. There was not a breath of wind blowing, and the air was calm and mild. Before he realized it, he had walked on for nearly three hours, and it was late in the night. But no sooner had he turned to head homeward than he heard the sound of voices and the trampling of feet coming toward him along the road.

"I don't know who can be out so late at night and on such a lonely road," said Teig to himself. He stopped to listen and heard the voices of many people talking to each other, but he could not understand what they were saying. "It's not Irish or English they're speaking," he said, "and it can't be that they're Frenchmen!" He went on a couple of yards farther, and he saw well enough by the light of the moon a band of little people coming towards him, carrying something big and heavy with them. "Och!" said he. "Sure it's the good people themselves!" Every rib of hair on his head stood up, for he saw that they were coming toward him fast despite their heavy load.

As they approached, he perceived that there were twenty little men in all, not a man of them higher than about three feet. But he could not make out what the heavy thing was that they were carrying until they reached him and stopped to stand in front of him. Then they threw the heavy thing down on the road, and he saw on the spot that it was a dead body.

He became cold then, and there was not a drop of blood running in his veins when one of the little men, old and grey, came up to him and said, "Isn't it lucky we met you, Teig O'Kane?"

Poor Teig could not have brought out a word at all if his life depended on it, and so he gave no answer.

"Teig O'Kane," said the little grey man again, "isn't it timely you met us?"

Teig could not answer him.

"Teig O'Kane," says he, "for the third time, isn't it lucky and timely that we met each other?"

But Teig remained silent, for his tongue was as if it was tied to the roof of his mouth.

The little grey man turned to his companions, and there was joy in his bright little eye. "And now," said he, "Teig O'Kane hasn't said a word, so we can do with him what we please. Teig," he said, "you're living a bad life. You've offended your father and jilted a girl who loves you. You're not unlike our man here, in fact, who lived a bad enough life himself," he said, gesturing at the corpse that lay on the ground. "But it just so happens we've a job to do tonight, and you're the man to help us with it. Now, lift that corpse."

Teig was frightened, but he was also obstinate as ever. "I won't," he said.

"Teig O'Kane won't lift the corpse," said the man with a wicked little laugh, like the striking of a cracked bell. "Make him lift it."

Almost before the words were out of his mouth, all the little men came running toward Teig, talking and laughing all the while. Teig tried to run from them, but they followed him, and one stretched out his foot before Teig as he ran, so that he was thrown in a heap on the road. Then, before he could rise up, the fairies caught him, some by the hands and some by the feet, and they held him tight with his face against the ground. He felt them laying something heavy across his back and throwing something around his neck. Then they stood back from him and let him get up.

He rose, foaming at the mouth and cursing. But his fear and wonder were great when he found that the things wound tight around his neck were a pair of bony, cold arms and the thing hanging off his back was the corpse itself. He shook himself and pried at the arms that were squeezing his neck, but however strongly he tried, he could not throw it off, any more than a horse can throw off its saddle. He was terribly frightened then, and he thought he was lost. "Och!" said he to himself. "It's the bad life I'm leading that has given the good people this power over me."

The little grey man came up to him again and said, "Now, Teig, you didn't lift the body when I told you to lift it, and see how you were made to lift it. Perhaps when I tell you to bury it, you won't bury it until you're made to bury it!"

"Anything at all that I can do for your honor," said Teig, "I'll do it." For he was getting some sense now.

The little man laughed his harsh laugh again. "You're getting quiet now, Teig," says he. "I'll wager you'll be quiet enough before I'm done with you. Listen to me now, and if you don't obey me in all I'm telling you to do, you'll repent it. You must carry this corpse that is on your back to the church of Teampoll-Démus, and you must bring it into the church with you, and make a grave for it in the very middle of the church. You must raise up the flagstones to dig the grave, and put them down again the very same way, and leave the place as it was when you came.

"But that's not all. Maybe the body won't be allowed to be buried in that church. Perhaps some other man has the bed, and, if so, it's likely he won't share it with this one. If you don't get leave to bury it in Teampoll-Démus, you must carry it to Carrick-fhad-vic-Orus and bury it there; and if you don't get it into that place, take it with you to Teampoll-Ronan; and if that place is closed on you, you've no more to do than to take it to Kill-Breedya, and you can bury it there without hindrance. I cannot tell you which one of those places is the one where you will have leave to bury that corpse under the clay, but I know that it will be one or another of them. If you do this work rightly, we will be thankful to you, and you will have no cause to grieve; but if you are slow or lazy, believe me, we shall take satisfaction of you."

When the grey little man had done speaking, his comrades laughed and clapped their hands together. "Go on, go on!" they all cried. "You have eight hours before you 'til daybreak, and if you haven't buried this man before the sun rises, you're lost." Then they struck at him with a fist and a foot, and drove him down the road.

Hours later, it seemed, Teig was still walking, and he thought to himself that there was not a wet path or crooked contrary road in the whole country that he had not walked that night. It was very dark, but sometimes the moon would break out clearly, and then he would look behind him and see the little people following at his back, talking amongst themselves in their strange language.

At last one of them cried out to him, "Stop here!"

He stood, and they all gathered around him.

"Do you see those withered trees over there?" said the little grey man. "Teampoll-Démus is among those trees. But you must go on by yourself, for we cannot follow you there. Go on boldly."

Teig looked and saw an old grey church with a dozen withered old trees scattered here and there around it. The old gate to the churchyard was thrown down, and he had no difficulty in entering. He turned then to see if any of the little people were following him, but there came a cloud over the moon, and the night became so dark that he could see nothing. So he went into the churchyard and walked up the old grassy pathway leading to the church. But when he reached the door, he found it locked.

"Now," he said to himself, "I have no more to do; the door is shut, and I can't open it."

Before these words were rightly shaped in his own mind, a voice in his ear said to him, "Search for the key on the top of the door."

He started and turned round. "Who is that speaking to me?" he cried, but he saw no one.

The voice said in his ear again, "Search for the key on the top of the door."

"What's that?" said he, the sweat running from his forehead. "Who spoke to me?"

"It's I, the corpse, that spoke to you," said the voice.

"Can you talk?" said Teig.

"Now and again," said the corpse.

With a trembling hand, Teig searched for the key, and he found it on the top of the door. He was too frightened to say any more, but he opened the door wide and went in with the corpse on his back. It was as dark as pitch inside.

"Light the candle," said the corpse.

Teig drew a flint steel and an old burnt rag out of his pockets. He struck a spark and lit the rag and blew it until it made a flame. The church, he could now see, was very ancient. The windows were blown in or cracked, and the timber of the seats was rotten. There were six or seven old iron candlesticks left there still, and in one of these candlesticks, Teig found the stump of an old candle and lit it with the burning rag. He was still looking around him at the strange and horrid place in which he found himself, when the cold corpse whispered in his ear, "Bury me now, bury me now. There is a spade to turn the ground."

Teig looked and saw a spade lying beside the altar. He took it up, placed the blade under a flagstone that was in the middle of the aisle, and, leaning all his weight on the handle of the spade, he raised the flag. When the first flag was raised, it was not hard to raise the others near it, and he moved three of them out of their places. The clay that was under them was soft and easy to dig, but he had not thrown up more than three shovelfuls when he felt the iron touch something softer than the clay. He threw up three or four more shovelfuls from around it, and then he saw that it was another body that was buried in the same place.

"I am afraid I'll never be allowed to bury the two bodies in the same hole," said Teig. "You, corpse, there on my back, will you be satisfied if I bury you down here?"

But the corpse didn't answer him a word.

"That's a good sign," said Teig to himself. "Maybe he's getting quiet." He thrust the spade down in the earth again.

Perhaps he hurt the flesh of the other body, for the dead man that was buried there stood up in the grave, and shouted an awful shout. "Go! Go! Go! Or you're a dead, dead, dead man!" And then he fell back in the grave again.

Teig's hair stood upright on his head like the bristles of a pig, the cold sweat ran off his face, and there came a tremor over all his bones. But when he saw that the second corpse lay quietly again, he became bolder and hurried to throw the clay back over it and lay down the flags carefully as they had been before. "It can't be that he'll rise up anymore," he said to himself.

He went down the aisle a little farther and began raising the flags again, looking for another bed for the corpse on his back. But he hadn't been digging very long before he laid bare an old woman. She was more lively than the first corpse, for he had scarcely taken any of the clay away from about her when she sat up and began to cry, "Ho, you clown! Where has he been that he got no bed?"

Poor Teig drew back, and when she found that she was getting no answer, she closed her eyes gently and fell back quietly and slowly under the clay. Quickly, Teig threw the clay back on her and put the flags down on top.

He moved down the aisle again and began to dig a third time, but before he had thrown up more than a couple of shovelfuls, he noticed a man's hand laid bare by the spade. "By my soul, I'll go no farther, then," said he to himself. And he threw the clay back down and settled the flags as they had been before.

He left the church then, his heart heavy, but he remembered to shut the door, lock it, and leave the key where he had found it on the top of the door. Then he was in great doubt as to what he should do next. He laid his face between his two hands and cried for grief and fatigue, for he was certain that he never would come home alive. He made another attempt to loosen the hands of the corpse that were squeezed round his neck, but the more he tried to loosen them, the tighter they squeezed him.

Then the cold, horrid lips of the dead man whispered in his ear, "Carrick-fhad-vic-Orus," and he remembered the command of the good people to bring the corpse there if he was unable to bury it in the first place.

He rose up and looked about him. "I don't know the way," he said.

As soon as he had uttered the words, the corpse stretched out its left hand and pointed to show him the road he ought to follow. Teig went in the direction that the fingers were stretched. He passed out of the church-yard and followed an old, rutty, stony road, and whenever he came to a path or road meeting it, the corpse always stretched out its bony hand and pointed, showing him the way he was to take.

At last he saw an old burying ground beside the road. There was neither church nor chapel nor any other building in it.

The corpse squeezed him tightly and said, "Bury me, bury me in the burying ground."

Teig stumbled toward the old burying ground, and he was not more than twenty yards from it when, raising his eyes, he saw hundreds and hundreds of ghosts—men, women, and children—sitting on top of the wall round about, standing at the gate, and running backwards and forwards inside. They were all pointing at him, and he could see their mouths opening and shutting as if they were speaking, though he heard no words.

He was afraid to go forward, so he stood where he was, and the moment he stood, all the ghosts became quiet and ceased moving. He walked a couple of yards forwards, and immediately the whole crowd rushed together towards the gate, and stood so thickly together that he never could break through them, even if he had a mind to try. But he had no mind to try it.

He went back to the road broken and dispirited and then stopped, for he did not know which way he was to go.

But the corpse whispered, "Teampoll-Ronan," and the skinny hand stretched out again, pointing down the road.

As tired as he was, Teig had nothing to do but walk. The road was neither short nor even, the night was darker than ever, and it was difficult to make his way. Many times he stumbled and fell, and many were the bruises he got. At last he saw Teampoll-Ronan in the distance, a crumbling church standing in the middle of a burying ground. He trudged towards it, and as he got near and saw no ghosts at the gate, he thought he was all right and safe. But as he was passing through it, he tripped on the threshold. Before he could recover himself, something that he could not see seized him by the neck, by the hands, and by the feet, and bruised him, and shook him, and choked him, until he was nearly dead. And at last he was lifted up and carried more than a hundred yards from that place, and then thrown down in an old ditch, with the corpse still clinging to him.

As he lay there, bruised and sore, the corpse said in his ear, "Kill-Breedya."

So Teig rose up and went on in the direction the corpse pointed out to him. The wind was cold, the road was bad, and the load upon his back was heavy. He could not have told how long he had been going when the dead man suddenly squeezed him and said, "There! Bury me there."

"This is the last burying place," said Teig, "and the little grey man said I'd be allowed to bury him in one of them, so it must be this one."

The first faint streak of the morning was appearing in the east, but it was darker than ever, for the moon was set and there were no stars.

"Make haste, make haste!" said the corpse.

Teig hurried forward to the graveyard, which was a little place on a bare hill, with only a few graves in it. He walked boldly in through the open gate, and nothing touched him. Then he looked around him for a spade or shovel to make a grave, but instead he saw something that startled him greatly: a newly-dug grave lay right before him.

He looked down into it, and there at the bottom he saw a black coffin. He clambered down into the hole and lifted the lid, and found that the coffin was empty. He had hardly done this when the corpse, which had clung to him for more than eight hours, suddenly relaxed its hold of his neck and sank down softly into the open coffin.

Teig made no delay then. He pressed the coffin lid down in its place and scrambled up out of the grave. He threw the clay over it with his two hands, and when the grave was filled up, he stamped and leaped upon it until it was firm and hard, and then he left the place.

The sun was rising fast, and he set out as quickly as his weary legs could carry him along the road. At last he came to an inn, where he would have dearly liked to take a rest. But he knew that his father—and Mary—were waiting for him to give his answer that very morning. So he hired a horse instead and rode home. He found that he was more than twenty-six miles from home, and he had come all that way with the dead body on his back in one night.

Teig was not a fortnight at home before he married Mary, and he was a happy man from that day forwards. He never drank too much, he never lost his money over cards, and, most especially, he would not for the world be out late by himself on a dark night.

4

ROMANCE

THE WITCH
of LOK ISLAND

Brittany

n olden times, when fairies were still commonplace in Brittany, there lived a young man called Yann and a maiden called Bella. They had grown up together and loved each other with all their hearts. And when their parents died, leaving them next to nothing, they became servants in the same house.

They ought to have been happy, but lovers are like the ever-moaning sea.

"If only we had enough to buy a little cow and a lean pig," said Yann, "I would hire a bit of land from our master. Then the priest would marry us and we could live together."

"Yes," replied Bella with a heavy sigh, "times are so hard. Cows and pigs were dearer than ever last week at the fair."

They complained thus every day until at last Yann became impatient. One morning he went to the threshing-floor where Bella was winnowing grain, and told her he was going to set out to seek his fortune. Bella tried her best to persuade him not to go. But he would not listen.

"Birds fly straight to the cornfield," said he, "and bees to the flowers for their honey. A man ought to have as much sense as winged creatures. I am going to find what I want, the price of a little cow and a lean pig. If you love me, Bella, you will not stand in the way of a plan that will bring about our marriage."

"Go with heaven's help then, if you must," said Bella, "but before you go, I want to give you the most precious treasures my parents left to me."

She led Yann to her linen press and took from it a silver pocketknife, a little gold bell, and an applewood staff. "These relics have never gone out of our family," she said. "Whatever this knife touches will escape from the spell of magician or of witch. The sound of this bell can be heard at any distance. It warns our friends of any danger we may be in. And lastly, this staff will guide the bearer to wherever he may wish to go. I give you the knife to defend you from evil spells, and the bell so that it may warn me when you are in danger. But I shall keep the staff, so that I shall be able to reach you if you need me."

Yann thanked his sweetheart. They shed a few tears together as they said their goodbyes, and then he started off to seek their fortune.

He traveled for several days across the land and over the mountains, until at last he reached a seaside town overlooking several islands. He spent the night at an inn there, and the next morning, as he was sitting at the door of the inn, he saw two salt dealers pass, leading their mules. Yann overheard them talking about the witch of Lok Island, who was richer than all the wealth of the kings of the world. Yann went to them and asked what they meant, and they answered that the witch of Lok Island was a fairy who lived in a lake in the middle of the biggest of the islands. They told Yann that many a rash lad in search of fortune had gone to the island to find her treasure but not one of them had ever returned.

When Yann heard this, he declared at once that he, too, would go to the island to seek the witch's treasure. The salt dealers tried to dissuade him, insisting that they could not let a young man go to certain rack and ruin, and they threatened to keep him back by force. Yann thanked them for the interest they showed in him, and said he was ready to give up the plan if they would pass the hat around and collect just enough money for him to buy a little cow and a lean pig. Whereupon they all changed their tune, saying that Yann was a stubborn-headed chap and that they could not stop him anyhow.

So Yann went down to the seashore and hailed a ferryman, who rowed him over to Lok Island. He soon found the pool in the middle of the island. It was surrounded with sea-drift covered with pale pink blossoms, and at the far end of the lake, in the shade of a clump of flowering broom, a sea-green boat was floating on the still water. The boat looked like a sleeping swan with its head under its wing.

Yann had never seen anything like it, and he drew near out of curiosity. Then he stepped into the boat to examine it more closely. Hardly had he set his foot in it than the swan awoke. Its head came out from under its feathers, its webbed feet spread out in the water, and suddenly it glided away from the shore.

The youth uttered a cry of dismay, but the swan only paddled more quickly toward the middle of the lake. Then, without warning, the bird put its bill in the water and plunged, carrying Yann into the depths.

At first Yann feared he would drown. But presently he realized he could breathe quite easily beneath the water. He opened his eyes and saw the witch's palace, which was built on the sandy bottom of the lake. It was made of seashells, lovelier than anything you can imagine. All around were immense gardens and lawns of seaweed, set with diamonds instead of flowers, and surrounding the gardens was a forest of sea trees.

The swan left Yann at the foot of a crystal stairway leading up to the door of the palace. He began to climb, and with each step he took, the stairs rang out with a sound like birdsong. At last Yann stood in the doorway of the palace, and there in the first room he saw the witch lying on a golden bed. She was dressed in sea-green silk as fine and soft as a wave. Coral ornaments adorned her black hair, which fell down to her feet. And her cheeks were as delicately tinted as the inside of a shell.

Yann drew back at the sight of so delightful a being. But the fairy rose up smiling and came toward him. Her walk was as graceful as the sweep of the waves on the rolling sea.

"Welcome," she said, motioning him to come in. "There is always a place here for strangers and handsome youths like you."

Yann felt bolder and entered the room.

"Who are you?" asked the witch. "And what do you want?"

"My name is Yann," said the boy, "and I am looking for enough money to buy a little cow and a lean pig."

"Very well," answered the witch with a smile. "Your search shall be rewarded, and you shall have your heart's desire."

She led him deeper into the palace, to a room whose walls were hung with threaded pearls, and gave him eight kinds of wine in eight golden goblets. Yann began by tasting the eight kinds of wine and, as he found them very nice, he drank eight times of each. And with each goblet he drank, he thought the witch was more and still more beautiful. Had the world ever seen so enchanting a being?

As he drank, she told him that her lake was connected by an underground passage with the sea, and that all the wealth of wrecked ships was drawn thither by a magic current.

"On my honor!" cried Yann, whom the wine had made jolly, "I am not surprised that landlubbers speak so badly of you. People as rich as you are always making others envious. As far as I am concerned, half your fortune would do for me."

"You shall have it, Yann," said the witch.

"But how can you manage that?" asked Yann, surprised.

"I have lost my husband," she answered, "and so if I am to your taste, I will be your wife."

The young man was quite breathless at what he heard. Was it possible that he was to marry the beautiful fairy whose palace was rich enough to contain eight barrels of marvelous wine? To be sure he had promised to marry Bella, but his memories of her were quickly becoming clouded by the fumes from the witch's wine.

So Yann told the fairy very politely that he could not refuse her offer, and that he was overcome with joy at the prospect of becoming her husband.

The witch then said she would prepare the feast for the betrothal at once. She set a table and spread it with the nicest foods Yann had ever laid eyes upon, as well as many he had never tasted before. Then she went out into the garden to a fish pond and, taking a net in her hand, leaned out over the water.

"Come hither, come hither, attorney general," she cried. "Come hither, come hither, O, miller! O, tailor! O, beadle!"

And each time she spoke a name, Yann could see a fish leap into her net. When the net was full, she came back into the palace and threw all four of the fish into a golden frying pan.

It seemed to Yann that amidst the sputter of the frying he could hear whispers.

"Who is whispering in your golden frying pan, fairy?" he asked.

"It's just the sparks that the wood is throwing out," she said, blowing up the fire.

But in a moment little voices began to mutter.

"Who is muttering?" asked the young man.

"It's just the fat that is melting," she replied, tossing up the fish in the pan.

But soon the voices began to shout.

"Who is shouting so, fairy?" asked Yann.

"It's just the cricket on the hearthstone," answered the witch, and she began singing so loudly that Yann could hear nothing else.

Now all that was happening was beginning to clear Yann's wits. But before he could make up his mind what to do, the witch brought in the fried fish and begged him to sit down to dinner. Then she said she would fetch twelve more kinds of wine for him to taste.

Yann sat down with a sigh and, without thinking, reached into his pocket for the silver knife Bella had given him, to cut the fish with. But at the sight of it, he felt a pang of remorse. "Mercy on us!" he said to himself. "Is it possible that I could forget Bella so soon for the sake of this devious witch?"

He set the knife down on his plate and started to stand up. But hardly had the spell-destroying knife touched the golden dish than all the fishes stood up and transformed before his eyes into little men. Each one wore the garb of his profession or trade. There was an attorney general with his white bib, a miller all covered with flour, a tailor in violet stockings, and a beadle in his surplice. And they all shouted out together as they hopped up and down in the hot frying fat: "Yann, save us if you wish to be saved yourself!"

"Holy saints! Who are all these little men singing in the melted butter?" cried Yann, dumbfounded.

"We are poor men like yourself," they shouted back. "We too came to Lok Island to seek our fortune. We agreed to marry the witch, and the day after the wedding she treated us just as she had treated those who came before us, and who are all now in the big fish pond. Soon you will be in the same state, perhaps even fried and eaten by the newcomers!" they cried.

Yann leaped up as though he were already in the golden frying pan himself. He rushed toward the door, hoping to escape before the witch came back. But she had slipped into the room and heard everything. Before Yann could reach the door she threw her steel net over him, and immediately poor Yann was turned into a frog. Then the witch threw him into the fish pond with her other enchanted husbands.

AT THAT VERY MOMENT THE LITTLE GOLDEN BELL that Yann wore around his neck gave forth a tinkling note, and far away, Bella heard it as clearly as if it had been hung around her own neck. "Yann is in danger," she cried. And with no more ado, without asking anyone's advice, she ran to her room, grasped the magic staff, and set off. When she reached the crossroads, she stuck her staff in the ground and murmured:

"O, staff of applewood so fair,
Lead me on land and through the air,
Above the cliffs and o'er the sea,
For with my lover I must be."

At her words, the staff transformed into a chestnut steed, completely saddled and bridled. He had a ribbon above each ear and a blue tassel on his forehead.

Bella mounted and off they went, first at a pace, then at a trot, and then at a gallop. At last they were traveling so swiftly that the trees and the ditches and the church steeples flew past the girl's eyes.

Yet she longed for ever more speed, and she urged her horse onward, whispering in his ear, "The horse is less swift than the swallow, the swallow is less swift than the wind, the wind is less swift than the lightning, but, steed of mine, you must be swifter than all, for the dearest half of my heart is in danger."

The horse understood her and flew like chaff blown before a gale.

At last they reached the foot of a sheer rock in the mountains that people call Hart's Leap Rock. There the swift steed came to a halt, for neither man nor beast has ever climbed that cloud-capped rock. But Bella repeated her rhyme:

"O, staff of applewood so fair,
Lead me on land and through the air,
Above the cliffs and o'er the sea,
For with my lover I must be."

Hardly had she finished the last line when wings grew out of the horse's flanks, and he became a mighty bird that bore her on the winds to the very summit of the cliff.

And at the top someone was waiting for her. Perched on a cold rock at the very summit was a little hobgoblin, withered and bearded. When he saw Bella, he shouted out, "Here is the fair maid who has come to save me!"

"To save you!" cried Bella. "Who are you?"

"I am Jennik, the ill-fated husband of the witch of Lok Island. She grew tired of me and trapped me here with her spells."

"Alas, poor thing!" exclaimed the maiden. "How can I deliver you?"

"Just as you will deliver Yann, who is in the witch's power," he replied.

"Ah, tell me what I must do!" cried Bella.

"You must go to the witch of Lok Island and introduce yourself as a young lad. Then you will be on the lookout for your chance to snatch the steel net she carries in her belt. Shut her in it and she will remain there 'til the end of time."

"Where can I get boys' clothes to fit me?" asked Bella.

"You will soon see, pretty maid." As he spoke, the hobgoblin pulled out four of his red hairs, blew upon them, and muttered something beneath his breath. Instantly the four hairs became four tailors. The first tailor held a cabbage in his hand, the second a pair of scissors, the third a needle, and the fourth a flatiron. Without more ado they sat themselves around the rock with their legs crossed, and began to make a young lad's suit for Bella. With the first cabbage leaf they made a fine-laced coat. Another leaf soon became the waistcoat, and it took two leaves to make the baggy trousers. Finally a hat was cut out of the heart of the cabbage, and the stalk was used to make the shoes.

When Bella had put on these clothes, she looked like a young nobleman, for her garments were of green velvet, lined with white satin.

"Haste! Haste!" cried the hobgoblin when he saw her ready for her adventure. "Away to rescue Yann!"

Bella quickly mounted her great bird, and in one swift flight he transported her to the lake in the middle of Lok Island. There she dismounted, and the bird became a simple staff of applewood once again. Immediately, Bella spied the swan boat, and, just like Yann, she stepped into it and was carried across the water and down to the bottom of the lake. She spared little time admiring the seashell palace, but ran up the sweetly singing stairs to the door, where she found the witch.

At the sight of the velvet-clad youth, the witch was delighted. "By all my gold and silver," she said to herself, "this is the handsomest lad I ever saw, and I think I shall love him for some time."

So she was all graciousness at once, calling Bella her beloved and leading her to the table, which was still beautifully set with all manner of good things. And there before her, Bella saw the magic knife that she had given Yann, and that he had left behind him as he had leaped toward the door.

Bella quickly took the knife and hid it in her pocket. Then, after she had politely tasted each of the delicious dishes spread across the table, the witch led her out into the garden to show her the lawns set with diamonds, the fountains with their lavender-scented sprays, and last of all the fish pond, where thousands of many-colored fish were swimming. Bella feigned delight and gazed with rapture on everything.

The witch was pleased and asked immediately if Bella would consent to marry her and live with her in the palace forever.

"Oh, yes indeed!" replied Bella. "But first let me try to catch one of those pretty fishes with the steel net you have at your belt."

The witch, thinking the request a mere whim of boyish fancy, smiled and handed Bella the net. "Now, fair fisherman," she said, "let us see what may be your luck. A rich catch may await you."

"I will catch an accursed witch!" cried Bella, quickly throwing the net over the witch's head.

The witch uttered one terrifying shriek that ended in a moan as Bella hastily rolled up the net and threw the witch into the middle of the fish pond. Then, as if the ripples from the splash were driving them out, the fish began to rise up and leave the water like a procession of many-colored monks. They piped out in their tiny voices, "Here is our lord and master who has delivered us from the steel net and the golden frying pan!"

"And who will also give you back your human form," said Bella, taking out the magic knife. And as she touched each of the fish in turn, they all became the young men they had been before the witch had ensnared them.

But as the young men rejoiced around her and Bella touched the last fish with her knife, she was downcast because Yann had not yet appeared. Then she noticed a large green frog at her feet. It was on its knees sobbing bitterly with its forepaws crossed upon its breast, and on a cord around its neck there hung a little golden bell. Bella felt her heart give a sudden bound, and she cried, "Is that you, my little Yann? Is that you, king of my joys and of my cares?"

"It is I," groaned the frog.

Then Bella touched him with the knife, and immediately Yann stood before her in his own true form. They kissed each other, laughing and crying all at once.

Just then, who should arrive, but the hobgoblin of Hart's Leap Rock. "Here I am, fair maid!" the hobgoblin called to Bella. "The spell is broken. May heaven shower blessings on you!"

Then he led them all to the witch's treasure chest. When they opened it they found that it was full of precious stones.

"There is enough for all," said the hobgoblin.

So both Bella and Yann filled their pockets, their hats, their belts, and even their wide trouser legs. When they had as many gems as they could carry, Bella ordered her staff of applewood to become a coach large enough to hold all the people she had set free.

Thus they returned home. At last their wedding banns were published, and Yann and Bella were married. But instead of buying a little cow and a lean pig, they bought all the fields in the parish and settled down as farmers, and they lived prosperous and happy for the rest of their lives.

THE BLACK BULL
of NORROWAY

Scotland

n bygone days, long centuries ago, there lived a widow who had four daughters. The widow was so poor and had fallen upon such evil days that she and her daughters often had much ado to get enough to eat. So the eldest daughter determined that she would set out into the world to seek her fortune, and her mother was quite willing that she should do so.

"For," said she, "'tis better to work abroad than to starve at home."

But as there was an old henwife living nearby who was said to be a witch and be able to foretell the future, the widow sent her daughter to the henwife's cottage, to ask in which of the four directions she ought to go in order to find the best fortune.

"You need go no farther than my back door, dear," answered the old dame, who had always felt very sorry for the widow and her pretty daughters, and was glad to do them a good turn.

So the eldest daughter ran through the passage to the henwife's back door and peeped out, and what should she see but a magnificent coach, drawn by six beautiful cream-colored horses, coming along the road. Greatly excited at this unusual sight, she hurried back to the kitchen and told the henwife what she had seen.

"Aweel, aweel, you've seen your fortune," said the old woman, in a tone of satisfaction, "for that coach-and-six is coming for you."

Sure enough, the coach-and-six stopped at the widow's door, and the second daughter came running down to the cottage to tell her sister to make haste because it was waiting for her. Delighted beyond measure at the wonderful luck that had come to her, she hurried home, said farewell to her mother and sisters, and took her seat within, and the horses galloped off immediately.

A few weeks afterwards, the second daughter thought that she would do as her sister had done and go down to the henwife's cottage. She told her that she, too, was going out into the world to seek her fortune. And of course, in her heart of hearts, she hoped that what had happened to her sister would happen to her also.

And, curious to say, it did. For the old henwife sent her to look out at her back door, and she went, and lo and behold, another coach-and-six was coming along the road. When she ran and told the old woman, she smiled upon her kindly and told her to hurry home, for the coach-and-six was her fortune also, and it had come for her. So the second daughter ran home, got into her grand carriage, and was driven away.

After that, the third daughter was eager to seek her fortune, too. And everything happened as before. The henwife sent her to look out the back door, she saw a coach-and-six approaching, and she didn't even pause to ask the old woman whether this was her fortune, but rushed straight home and into the coach that was awaiting her.

Of course with all these lucky happenings, the youngest daughter, whose name was Innes, was anxious to try what her fortune might be. So that very night, in high good humor, she tripped away down to the old witch's cottage.

She, too, was told to look out at the back door, and she was only too glad to do so, for she fully expected to see a fourth coach-and-six coming rolling along the high road. But alas and alack! No such sight greeted her eager eyes, for the high road was quite deserted, and in great disappointment she ran back to the henwife to tell her so.

"Then it is clear that your fortune is not coming to meet you this day," said the old dame, "so you must come back tomorrow."

Innes went home again, and next day she turned up once more at the henwife's cottage. But once more she was disappointed, for although she looked out long and eagerly, no glad sight of a coach-and-six or of any other coach greeted her eyes. And the henwife told her to come back again the next day.

On the third day, when Innes looked out the back door, what should she see but a great black bull coming rushing along the road, bellowing as it came, and tossing its head fiercely in the air. In great alarm, she shut the door and ran to the henwife to tell her about the furious animal that was approaching.

"Oh, dear," cried the old woman, holding up her hands in dismay. "Who would have thought that the Black Bull of Norroway was to be your fate!"

At those words, the poor little maiden grew pale. She had come out to seek her fortune, but it had never dawned upon her that her fortune could be anything so terrible as this. "But the bull cannot be my fortune," she cried in terror. "I cannot go away with a bull."

"But you'll need to," replied the henwife calmly. "For you looked out of my door with the intent of meeting your fortune, and when your fortune has come to you, you must follow it."

When the poor girl ran weeping to her mother to beg to be allowed to stay at home, she found her mother of the same mind as the old wise woman. So she allowed herself to be lifted up onto the back of the enormous black bull, which had come up to the door and was now standing there quietly enough. And when she was settled, he set off again on his wild career while she sobbed and trembled with terror, and clung to his horns with all her might.

On and on they went, until at last the poor girl was so faint with fear and hunger that she could scarce keep her seat. Just as she was losing her hold of the great beast's horns, however, and feeling that she must fall to the ground, he turned his massive head round a little, and, speaking in a wonderfully soft and gentle voice, he said, "Eat out of my right ear, and drink out of my left ear, so you will be refreshed for the journey."

So she put a trembling hand into the bull's right ear and drew out some bread and meat, which, in spite of her terror, she was glad to swallow. Then she put her hand into his left ear and found there a tiny flagon of wine, and when she had drunk that, her strength returned to her in a wonderful way.

Long they went and sore they rode until, just as it seemed to Innes that they must be getting near the world's end, they came in sight of a magnificent castle.

"That's where we may bide this night," said the bull, "for that is the house of one of my brothers."

The girl was greatly surprised at these words, but by this time she was too tired to wonder very much at anything, so she did not answer, but sat quietly until the bull ran into the courtyard of the castle and knocked his great head against the door.

The door was opened at once by a very splendid footman, who treated the bull with great respect and helped Innes to alight from his back. The bull trotted off quite contentedly to the grassy park which stretched all around the building, to spend the night there. Then the footman ushered the girl into a magnificent hall, where the lord of the castle and his lady were waiting. And who should the lady be but Innes's eldest sister.

The sisters were overjoyed to be reunited. They had a sumptuous supper, and then Innes was given a richly furnished bedroom, all hung round with golden mirrors. When she asked her sister about the bull, she could tell her nothing more than what she already knew. But in the morning, just as the bull came trotting up to the front door, the lord of the castle handed Innes a beautiful apple, telling her not to break it, but to put it in her pocket and keep it until she was in the direst strait that she had ever been in. Then she was to break it, and it would bring her out of trouble.

So Innes put the apple in her pocket, they lifted her once more onto the black bull's back, and she and her strange companion continued on their journey. All that day they traveled, and at night they came in sight of another castle, which was even bigger and grander than the first.

"That's where we may bide this night," said the bull, "for that is the home of another of my brothers."

To Innes's amazement, the lady of this castle was her second sister, and they rejoiced to be together again. Here she rested for the night in a very fine bedroom indeed, all hung with silken curtains, and the lord and her sister did everything to please her and make her comfortable, although they told her no more about the bull.

In the morning, before she left, they presented her with the largest pear that she had ever seen, and warned her that she must not break it until she was in the direst strait that she had ever been in, and then, if she broke it, it would bring her out of trouble.

The third day was the same as the other two had been. Innes and the bull rode many a weary mile, and at sundown they came to another castle, more splendid by far than the other two. This castle belonged to the bull's third brother, and here the girl was happy to find her third sister. And this time, when she departed the next morning, she received a most lovely plum, with the warning not to break it until she was in the direst strait that she had ever been in. Then she was to break it, and it would set her free.

On the fourth day, however, things were changed. There was no fine castle waiting for them at the end of their journey. Instead, as the shadows began to lengthen, they came to a dark, deep glen, which was so gloomy that the poor girl felt her courage sinking as they approached it.

At the entrance, the bull stopped. "Light down here, lady," he said, "for in this glen a deadly conflict awaits me, which I must face unaided and alone. The dark and gloomy region that lies before us is the abode of a great spirit of darkness, who works much ill in the world. I must fight with him and overcome him, and I have good hope that I shall do so. As for you, you must seat yourself on this stone and stir neither hand nor foot nor tongue 'til I return. For, if you so much as move, then the evil spirit of the glen will have you in his power."

"But how will I know what is happening to you," asked Innes anxiously, for she was beginning to grow quite fond of the huge black creature that had carried her so gallantly these last three days, "if I can move neither hand nor foot, nor even speak?"

"You will know by the signs around you," answered the bull. "For if everything about you turns blue, then you will know that I have vanquished the evil spirit, but if everything about you turns red, then the evil spirit has vanquished me."

So she sat, and the bull disappeared into the wood. It was hard work to sit still so long, but when she had sat there for well-nigh an hour, a curious change began to pass over the landscape. First it turned grey, and then it turned a deep azure blue, as if the sky had descended on earth.

"The bull has conquered," thought Innes. "Oh! What a noble animal he is!" And in her relief and delight she forgot to sit still, and she turned her head to look into the wood and see if the bull were coming back.

In a moment, a mystic spell fell upon her, which caused her to become invisible to the eyes of the Knight of Norroway, who, having vanquished the evil spirit, was loosed from the spell which had lain over him and had transformed him into the likeness of a great black bull. He was returning in haste down the glen to present himself, in his rightful form, to the maiden whom he loved and whom he hoped to win for his bride, but he could not see her. Long, long he sought, but he could not find her, while all the time she was sitting patiently waiting on the stone. For the spell was on her eyes, too, and hindered her from seeing him, as it hindered him seeing her.

On and on she sat on the stone, until at last she became so wearied and lonely and frightened, that she burst out crying and cried herself to sleep. When she woke in the morning, she felt that it was no use sitting there any longer, so she rose and went on her way.

SHE WANTED TO GO BACK TOWARDS HER SISTERS' CASTLES, but they had traveled so far from there that she could not tell which way to go. So she wandered until at last she came to a great hill made all of glass, which blocked her way and prevented her from going any farther. She could not remember passing it before, and she was about to turn around and walk back the way she had come, when she saw a little cottage at the bottom of the hill. She was exhausted, so she approached the cottage in hope of a place to rest for the night, or at least some advice on which way to go.

Beside the cottage there was a smithy where an old smith was working at his anvil. Innes entered the smithy and asked him, "What place is this?"

The old man laid down his hammer and looked at her. "This is the Mountain of Glass, lassie," he said. "On the other side of it lies the land of Norroway."

At this Innes's heart leaped, for she felt sure that if she could reach the other side of this mountain, she would be reunited with the bull, and something in her was still compelled to follow her fortune wherever it would lead. "That is where I wish to go," she said. "But how can I cross the mountain to the other side?"

"There is no easy road over the mountain," said the smith. "Folk either walk round it, which is not an easy thing to do, for the foot of it stretches out for hundreds of miles, and the folk who try to do so are almost sure to lose their way; or they walk over the top of it, and that can only be done by those who are shod with iron shoes."

"And how am I to get these iron shoes?" cried Innes eagerly. "Could you fashion me a pair, good man? I would gladly pay you for them." Then she stopped suddenly, for she remembered that she had no money.

"These shoes cannot be made for money," said the old man solemnly. "They can only be earned by service. I alone can make them, and I make them for those who are willing to serve me."

"And how long must I serve you before you make them for me?" she asked faintly.

"Seven years," replied the old man, "for they be magic shoes, and that is the magic number."

So, as there seemed nothing else for it, she hired herself to the smith for seven long years, to clean his house, cook his food, and make and mend his clothes. At the end of that time he fashioned her a pair of iron shoes, with which she climbed the Mountain of Glass with as much ease as if it had been covered with fresh green turf.

When she had descended to the other side, the first house that she came to was the house of an old washerwoman, who lived there with her only daughter. As Innes was very tired, she went up to the door, knocked, and asked if she might be allowed to rest there for the night.

The washerwoman, who had a sly face, said that she might, but on one condition. And that was that she should try to wash a white mantle that the Black Knight of Norroway had brought to her to wash, as he had got it stained in a deadly fight.

"Yesterday I spent the live-long day washing it," said the old dame, "and I might as well have let it lie on the table. For at night, when I took it out of the washtub, the stains were there as dark as ever. Peradventure, maiden, if you will try your hand upon it, you may be more successful. For I am loathe to disappoint the Knight, who is an exceeding great and powerful prince."

"Is he in any way connected with the Black Bull of Norroway?" asked Innes, for it seemed that maybe she was going to find once more him whom she had lost.

The old woman looked at her suspiciously. "The two are one," she answered, "for the Black Knight chanced to have a spell thrown over him, which turned him into a black bull, and which could not be lifted until he had fought with and overcome a mighty spirit of evil that lived in a dark glen. He fought with the spirit and overcame it, and once more regained his true form. But 'tis said that his mind is somewhat clouded at times, for he speaks ever of a maiden whom he would have wedded and whom he has lost. Though who or what she was, no living person kens. But this story can have no interest to a stranger like you," she added quickly, as if she were sorry for having said so much. "I have no more time to waste in talking. But if you will try to wash the mantle, you are welcome to a night's lodging; and if not, I must ask you to go on your way."

Needless to say, Innes said that she would try to wash the mantle, and it seemed as if her fingers had some magic power in them, for as soon as she put it into water, the stains vanished and it became as white and clean as when it was new.

Of course, the old woman was delighted, but she was very suspicious as well. For it appeared to her that there must be some mysterious link between the maiden and the Knight, if his mantle became clean so easily when she washed it, after the woman and her daughter had bestowed so much labor upon it and had not succeeded in getting it clean.

So, as she knew that the Black Knight intended to return for the mantle that very night, and as she wanted her daughter to get the credit for washing it, she advised Innes to go to bed early, in order to get a good night's rest after all her labors. The girl followed her advice, and so she was fast asleep, hidden in the big box bed in the corner, when the Black Knight of Norroway came to the cottage to claim his white mantle.

Now the young man had carried this mantle about with him for the last seven years—ever since his encounter with the evil spirit of the glen—and was always trying to find someone who could wash it for him, but never succeeding. For it had been revealed to him by a wise woman that she who could make it white and clean was destined to be his wife and that, moreover, she would prove a loving, faithful, and true wife.

So when he came to the washerwoman's cottage and received back his mantle white as the driven snow, and when he heard that it was the washerwoman's daughter who had wrought this wondrous change, he said at once that he would marry her the very next day.

When Innes awoke in the morning and heard all that had befallen, her heart was like to break. For now she felt that she never would have the chance of speaking to him and telling him who she really was.

In her sore distress, she suddenly remembered the beautiful fruit which she had received on her journey seven long years before, and which she had carried with her ever since.

"Surely I will never be in a sorer strait than I am now," she said to herself, and she drew out the apple and broke it. And lo and behold, it was filled with the most beautiful precious stones that she had ever seen. At the sight of them, a plan came suddenly into her head.

She took the precious stones out of the apple and, putting them into a corner of her kerchief, carried them to the washerwoman. "See," said she, "I am richer than maybe you thought I was. And all these riches may be yours."

"And how could that come about?" asked the old woman eagerly, for she had never seen so many precious stones in her life before, and she dearly wished to become the possessor of them.

"Only put off your daughter's wedding for one day," replied Innes, "and let me watch beside the Black Knight as he sleeps tonight, for I have long had a great desire to see him."

To her astonishment the washerwoman agreed to this request. The wily old woman was very anxious to get the jewels, which would make her rich for life, and it did not seem to her that there was any harm in the girl's request. But she made up her mind that she would give the Black Knight a sleeping draught, which would effectually prevent him from speaking to this strange maiden. So she took the jewels and locked them up in her chest, and the wedding was put off.

That night, Innes slipped into the Black Knight's apartment when he was asleep, and watched all through the long hours by his bedside, singing this song to him in the hope that he would awake and hear it:

"Seven long years I served for thee,
The glassy hill I climbed for thee,
The mantle white I washed for thee,
And wilt thou not waken and turn to me?"

But although she sang it over and over again, as if her heart would burst, he neither listened nor stirred, for the old washerwoman's potion had made sure of that.

Next morning, in her great trouble, Innes broke open the pear, hoping that its contents would help her better than the contents of the apple had done. But in it she found just what she had found before, a heap of precious stones. Only they were richer and more valuable than the others had been.

So, as it seemed the only thing to do, she carried them to the old woman and bribed her to put the wedding off for yet another day and allow her to watch that night also by the Black Knight's bedside.

And the washerwoman did so. "For," she said to herself as she locked away the stones, "I shall soon grow quite rich at this rate."

But, alas, it was all in vain that Innes spent the long hours singing with all her might:

"Seven long years I served for thee,
The glassy hill I climbed for thee,
The mantle white I washed for thee,
And wilt thou not waken and turn to me?"

For the young prince whom she watched so tenderly remained deaf and motionless as a stone.

By the morning she had almost lost hope, for there was only the plum remaining now, and if that failed, her last chance had gone. With trembling fingers, she broke it open and found inside another collection of precious stones, richer and rarer than the others.

She ran with these to the washerwoman, and, throwing them into her lap, told her she could keep them all if she would put off the wedding once again and let her watch by the prince for one more night. And, greatly wondering, the old woman consented.

Now it chanced that the Black Knight, tired with waiting for his wedding, went out hunting that day with all his attendants behind him. And as the servants rode they talked together about something that had puzzled them sorely these two nights gone by. At last an old huntsman rode up to the Knight, with a question upon his lips.

"Master," he said, "we would fain ken who the sweet singer is who sings through the night in your chamber?"

"Singer!" the prince repeated. "There is no singer. My chamber has been as quiet as the grave, and I have slept a dreamless sleep ever since I came to stay at the cottage."

The old huntsman shook his head. "Taste not the old wife's draught this night, Master," he said earnestly. "Then you will hear what other ears have heard."

At other times the Black Knight would have laughed at his words, but the man spoke with such earnestness that he could not but listen to them. So that evening, when the washerwoman, as was her wont, brought the sleeping draught of spiced ale to his bedside, he told her that it was not sweet enough for his liking. When she turned and went to the kitchen to fetch some honey to sweeten it, he jumped out of bed and poured it all out of the window, and when she came back he pretended that he had drunk it after all.

So it came to pass that he lay awake that night, and heard Innes enter his room, and listened to her plaintive song, sung in a voice that was full of sobs:

"Seven long years I served for thee,
The glassy hill I climbed for thee,
The mantle white I washed for thee,
And wilt thou not waken and turn to me?"

And when he heard the song, he understood it all. He sprang up, took her in his arms, kissed her, and asked her to tell him the whole story. And when he heard it, he was so angry with the old washerwoman and her deceitful daughter that he ordered them to leave the country at once. Then he and Innes were married, and they lived happily all their days.

MEREDYDD
and THE WYVERN

—

Wales

he people of Coed-y-Moch were always in fear. Never for a single moment, night or day, could they shake off the alarm which hung about them like a cloud. At night they cowered in their houses with their hands pressed to their ears to shut out the heartrending screams which seemed to cut the darkness like a jagged knife. When day poured its cheering light upon the world, there was no respite from this terrible panic. For, even in broad daylight, their tormentor lay in evil ambush for any who might, perchance, approach its gruesome haunt. With a sudden, cruel movement, it would seize in silence upon its victim, crush life from the writhing limbs, and bear away the inanimate form for food. The whole valley lay under this baleful influence and, like weary captives, looked longingly for a daybreak which should bring deliverance.

The cause of all this misery was a loathsome winged snake called a wyvern. Sometimes the monster lay and sunned itself upon the pebbly shores of Cynwch Lake, with its slimy folds all uncoiled, gazing with a lackluster look across the dancing waves. At times one could see it creeping with hateful, stealthy movements, here and there upon the fertile slopes of Moel Othrum, jerking its cumbersome form into uncanny humps as it made its way in quest of food, and leaving a slimy track behind it.

The hunger of the loathly creature passed the comprehension of a man. With a huge, gaping mouth and cavernous belly, the wyvern seemed to have no limit to its powers of digestion, and its wings would beat with lazy enjoyment as it lay and chewed the meat of its choice. Sometimes, in its greed, it would swallow a lamb in one gulp. At other times, when it killed a beast, it bore the carcass to a tree, twined its eager length around both beast and tree trunk, and by coiling round and round, closer and closer, it crushed the animal to a pulp. Then, with slow motion of its slavering jaws, the wyvern sucked the goodness from its raw food. And at yet other times, when it did not want flesh, it stole the fruit of the trees, and with its long and whitish tongue stripped the orchards almost bare.

It flew over the valley at night and screamed with soul-stirring anguish, so that men shuddered to hear the sound. Its wings beat the air with a dull flap, like the flight of an owl. Its glowing, greenish eyes had keen and penetrating sight, and often, when flying high in the air, the wyvern would swoop suddenly down upon some unprotected fold of sheep, or upon a traveler wandering in the darkness, and a startled scream, only too quickly smothered, would tell of another victim.

In vain the people of the valley offered great rewards for the destruction of the wyvern. One cunning old wizard, called Llywelyn, strove earnestly to put an end to these terrible sufferings. For many nights and days he pondered and tried to devise a means to slay the wyvern. When the Lord of Nannau cried that he would give threescore head of cattle to whoever slew the evil creature, this clever old man strove even more eagerly to win the wealth. But all his efforts were unavailing. The woeful wailing still pierced the night, and by day the distant form of the wyvern spread menace from the mountainside. To make matters worse, the wyvern was growing older and more wary, and to entrap it or slay it became daily a task of greater difficulty.

Finally, the wizard Llywelyn made a bold bid for its blood. Wales had long been famous for its archers, so old Llywelyn hired a dozen of the keenest, whose arrows sped from the bow as a lightning flash speeds from the dark clouds upon the trembling earth, and he placed them on various points of vantage around the valley. Yet it was never possible to catch even a glimpse of the wyvern on the days when the bowmen were waiting. It was as though some subtle knowledge bade it beware. So Llywelyn's plan came to naught, and the wyvern still screamed through the darkness of the night.

Now there lived among the shepherds of the mountains a youth called Meredydd, whose heart leaped at the thought of the three-score cows that the Lord of Nannau had offered. He was not yet twenty-one years old, but was strong and sturdy beyond the average. By the strength of his hands alone he tore open the gaping mouths of wolves, or wrenched the deep-seated bough from the parent tree. At wrestling none was his equal, for, when the spirit was strong in his heart, he had the strength of many men and held his adversary like a little child in his grasp. Yet Meredydd was gentle and used his strength only for righteous purposes, and the thought of the wyvern burned in his brain red-hot, giving him no rest by day or night.

So he came down from the mountains to try to slay the monster. But he said nothing of his intentions, for he feared failure and wished for people not to know of his plan until it was accomplished. He told the secret to only one person, the fair Elwyn. They had met by chance one misty day on the mountain, when he was searching for a lost sheep and had slipped and fallen into a deep crevasse. She had come upon him and, with tireless patience, had dug him out and cleared a path for him to escape. Now, when he told her of his plan, so modest was he that a blush came to his swarthy cheek. But when Elwyn saw him blush, she knew that this purpose was indeed strong in Meredydd's heart, and that she could say nothing to dissuade him, although she loved him with all the tenderness of the springtide of life.

Elwyn, therefore, bent low her fair face until her golden hair hid the smile of pride on her lips, and said simply, "Go, Meredydd, and my thought and my heart will keep constant company with your absence."

So they parted. Meredydd traveled beyond the haunts of men, while Elwyn returned to her kinsfolk, who dwelled in Hafodfraith.

Meredydd's path was long and his heart heavy, but the bright, blue eyes of Elwyn shone before him like two guardian angels beckoning him onward. He thought, too, of the threescore cows, and in his mind he heard their lowing as they came home at nightfall to be milked. He thought of the little white farmhouse which stood vacant on the mountain yonder, and peopled it with many a pleasant thought as he strode onward.

On his way, he passed by the Monastery of the Standard, whose residents knew Meredydd and loved his merry face and valiant form. He turned in at the gates, passed up to the entrance, and blew loudly upon the horn to tell of his arrival. Then the kindly old priests of the monastery thronged hastily around him, asking for news and pressing him to take refreshments. So he sat and talked and ate the food they placed before him.

"Friends," he said before he departed, "trust me and help me in my hour of need. You are kindly and know the thoughts that assail the heart of youth. I go on a quest and need your prayers. So pray for me, but lend me also the glittering axe which fell from heaven, and which rests beneath your altar."

Then the priests guessed his resolve to kill the wyvern. The worthy old abbot said nothing, but rose and fetched the axe. It was carved with mystic words and was said to have fallen from heaven because, long since, it was found one morning quivering in the oaken door of the monastery, and none knew whence it came. He placed the weapon in the shepherd's hands and said, "Go, and our prayers shall rise urgently to the throne of heaven. For you go upon the errand of mercy."

Meredydd set out again, and before long before he lit upon the trail of the wyvern—a trail which lay like a band of death along the hillside. It was near Cynwch Lake that he saw the trail, and he followed it cunningly and speedily, up the hill-slopes and through the young woods, until he came to the open pastures beyond. There, with its slithering coils all limp in sleep, on the other side of a milk-white hawthorn hedge, lay the hateful wyvern. So vile was the appearance that Meredydd's heart stopped beating at the sight. But he remembered gentle Elwyn and the kindly priests, and he stole cautiously towards the monster's horrid head.

Now as Meredydd had left the monastery, he had not noticed that the cunning eye of Llywelyn the wizard watched him from his old hut. Reading resolution in the young shepherd's bearing, Llywelyn had tracked Meredydd from afar and now waited to see what would happen. For he still coveted the rich reward that would fall to the slayer of the wyvern.

But Meredydd, thinking only of his lofty purpose, took no notice. He was trying to guess how deeply the monster was asleep. He felt, with skillful thumb, the keen edge of the axe, and knew that it would not fail him. Then the knowledge sped into his brain that the hawthorn was one mass of bloom, and that nothing on the wide earth could make the wyvern so drunken with rich, swooning sleep as the heavy odor of that fragrant flower. So his plans grew clearer in his mind, the cold sweat of fear dried upon him, and he felt that victory was surely his.

He crept along the near side of the hedge until he found an opening near the wyvern's head. As he peeped through the gap, one baleful, green eye unclosed its lazy lid and looked venomously upon him. But sleep closed up the monster's brain again, and Meredydd crept out to deal the fatal blow. As he passed by the wyvern's snout, its pestilential breath came forth in a sigh, and Meredydd well-nigh sank to his knees before its hateful stench and the heat of its passage. But he recovered, rose to his full height, and, with the muscles of his arms straining like steel rods under the grip of his hands upon the haft of the axe, he struck a blow that sent an echo throbbing over the hillside, and the head of the wyvern fell asunder at his feet.

But Meredydd was still in peril. The death agonies of that enormous body were not easy to avoid, and he could not leap aside before the writhing tail caught him with cruel force and knocked him down upon the grass. Then, as he lay motionless and white as death, the crouching figure of Llywelyn crept upon the scene. Rapidly he took in what had occurred, and mad jealousy seized him. Since he had failed to slay the wyvern, he resolved that misery should dog the steps of the youth whose courage had surpassed his own skill and witchcraft. But, as he stepped forth to do a vile deed, he saw that Meredydd opened his eyes and raised himself upon his elbow. So Llywelyn withdrew to the shelter of the wood, shaking with rage, and casting in his mind how to bring evil upon the shepherd lad.

Meredydd slowly raised himself to his feet. A chill as of death swept over him, and he knew not whether he lived or was dead, but his heart revived as he looked on the wyvern and recollected the rewards he would receive and share with Elwyn. So he cut out the monster's tongue as a token of victory, and bore this and the axe to the good priests of the Monastery of the Standard.

They gave him wine, bid him rest, and made haste to carry the good news far and wide to the people of Coed-y-Moch. By nightfall, hundreds of rejoicing eyes gazed greedily upon the hated form of the wyvern, and the people praised the shepherd youth who had delivered them from its thrall. Men wondered at the power of the blow that had cloven that enormous skull. They measured out the wyvern's length and marveled at the sharp-pointed wings now drooping in the black, oozy blood which fell in heavy gouts from the wound and flowed slowly down the slope of the hill. The following morning, they dug a mighty grave and with great difficulty dragged the huge winged snake to its depths. And above the grave they built a cairn to mark the spot where Meredydd won his victory.

But at the Monastery of the Standard, Meredydd lay at death's door. Many a visitor called to see their deliverer, but the priests told how the wyvern's poison had entered the blood of the shepherd lad, so that he lay unconscious and spoke words which had no meaning.

Llywelyn came among the others and asked for news. He was met by the abbot, whose eye could read all secrets. When he told Llywelyn how grievously the fever held Meredydd, a baleful gleam of triumph appeared in the wizard's eyes. The old abbot saw it and knew the dangers that beset Meredydd's path. Still, he gave a courteous welcome to the wizard and praised him for his attempts to slay the wyvern, so that Llywelyn departed well-satisfied from the monastery.

But as Llywelyn paced down the path and out of the monastery, the abbot watched him sadly. Shaking his head, he murmured, "'Tis well the lad bides with us, but are there others whom Llywelyn can injure? Time will show. Aye, time will show us everything."

So the good priests of the Monastery of the Standard watched carefully over Meredydd and brought him safely through his illness. They knew of medicinal herbs, they insisted on rest, and they fed him with good homely fare until his blood flowed rich and free once more. Then the word went round that Meredydd was restored, and the people came to bring him his gifts. The Lord of Nannau came himself and placed the prize of threescore of cattle under the charge of the priests until the shepherd youth could take them home. So many gifts were there that Meredydd knew that from henceforth he was no longer a poor shepherd, but could take his place among the great people of the district.

But amid the feasting and revelry which followed the death of the hateful winged snake, Meredydd's heart was loyal to the past, and as soon as he grew strong enough to move his limbs freely, he longed to visit Elwyn.

What was she thinking about his deed? Did she wonder at his absence? Why had no message come from her? Yet, before Meredydd left the monastery, the old abbot led him aside and whispered words of caution, bidding him be on his guard against treachery.

On his way to seek Elwyn, Meredydd passed blithely over the road he had traversed to encounter the wyvern. Then the future was unknown and his intentions were buried in his heart; now his name was on everybody's lips, and wealth had poured in by reason of his bravery. But just as before, the vision of Elwyn shone clearly in his mind, and he longed earnestly to see her once more. One word of praise from her was worth all the world.

As he drew near to Elwyn's house, he could almost hear his heart beating, so deep was his emotion. But her parents met him before he reached the door, and told him that the maiden was away from home.

"And why have you not been here before this, Meredydd?" asked Elwyn's mother.

Meredydd looked at her in astonishment. "I could not come," he replied, "for I have been ill, and the priests of the Monastery of the Standard have been restoring me to life."

The parents exchanged glances, and they began to realize that the stories they had been told were false. The three of them stood and talked long and earnestly about the events which had occurred, and, as they spoke, the matter grew clearer. Someone must have spread a wrong report. It had been told at Hafodfraith that Meredydd had gone to spend his time in feasting and dancing among the people of Coed-y-Moch, and had forgotten his home and former friends. In bitter sorrow, Elwyn had gone away to spend her lonely days at her sister's home, far away beyond the mountain. So Meredydd, with her parents' advice, departed at once to seek her there.

But at the house of Elwyn's sister he was once more disappointed. Elwyn had set out for her home and should have arrived there by that time.

Meredydd turned away and, without waiting a moment, bent his steps back towards Hafodfraith.

A thick white mist had fallen like the skirts of a giant's robe over the heads of the mountains, and it rolled ever lower as the night advanced. A strange foreboding tore at Meredydd's heart, making the way weary and long. But had he known all, his anxiety would have been increased tenfold.

Elwyn had not arrived home, for Llywelyn had used his magic arts and the thick mist to lure her far from her path. All through the day she had striven to retrace her steps, but her confusion increased as her strength grew less, and after many weary, lonely hours, she sank down sadly upon a flat rock and sobbed bitterly.

As she sat sorrow-stricken, a mountain bird flew down to a crag nearby and uttered a frightened, plaintive cry.

"Poor bird," said Elwyn. "What anguish stirs your heart?"

She rose and followed the bird as it flew away. Once more it settled and gave its sorrowful cry, so she strove to approach it. Again the bird flew ahead, and thus she followed, until the mist enwrapped her, and amid pathless ways she heard naught save the cry of the bird. Suddenly her foot sank into a soft yielding spot, and she realized too late that she was trapped in a morass. Despite all her efforts, exhausted as she already was, Elwyn was unable to get clear.

As she struggled thus, Llywelyn appeared like a phantom out of the mist and, with an evil leer, told her that Meredydd was unfaithful to her, that he was at Coed-y-Moch, feasting and merrymaking with the people, and made much of by the maidens. "Aye, and it is said," Llywelyn added, "that his heart has gone out to the fair daughter of the Lord of Nannau, and that the wedding will soon take place." Then he disappeared, leaving Elwyn alone on the bleak mountainside, still more solitary and afraid.

She thought of Meredydd and her home in Hafodfraith. The sunny days of the past rose to her mind, and she dwelled with gladness on the comradeship she had enjoyed with Meredydd. Why had he so easily forgotten her? Then she thought of her old parents and burst into tears when she considered how lonely they would be without her.

"Oh! Meredydd, Meredydd!" she wailed. "Why did you go away?"

As she spoke, it seemed to her that a distant noise broke the silence which lay around her. Was it only her imagination? The air grew rapidly colder as she listened in vain, and she had now sunk to her knees in the morass. Yet, once again, she strove to cry aloud. "Meredydd, Meredydd!"

Then, indeed, there came an answering cry from someone shouting with all his might, "Elwyn! Elwyn!"

With all her remaining strength, she replied, "Here! Here! Come quickly!"

As he had pursued his sad way homeward, Meredydd had determined to win Elwyn back, come what might. He would go and tell her of his victory over the wyvern, and explain how it was won for her alone. She would see his rewards, the threescore of cattle and all the other gifts. With these thoughts in his mind, he had hurried on, but in his haste he had missed his way and soon found himself wandering on the wild wastes of the mountains. Then in his loneliness he had cried, "Elwyn! Elwyn!" And through the somber stillness that enwrapped him, as if in answer to his wild cry, he had thought he heard the distant voice of the one whom he loved so dearly. He had paused and listened, with his heart beating wildly. How could it be Elwyn in this wild and lonely place? Again he had heard the faint cry, and recognized the agony in the voice. He sprang forward then, searching wildly until he came to the edge of the morass and saw Elwyn's sad plight.

He leaned over and, with the utmost gentleness, using every care, dragged her from the place which she had thought would be her grave. Although she was half-dead, yet she was life itself to Meredydd. Even as the sun in spring brings back life to the chilled and sleeping trees, so the very sight of Elwyn inspired him with the resolution to bring her safely home. He rubbed her cold hands, wrapped her warmly in his shepherd's plaid, and, holding her like a child in his strong young arms, passed heedfully down the mountain slope. A shepherd's hut gave them shelter for the night, and when the day broke the mist had rolled away. They could see the distant path leading like a long, grey silken thread over the mountains to Hafodfraith.

By the time they reached Elwyn's home, all had been explained and they knew the cunning arts that had separated them. Then Meredydd recalled the earnest words of the old abbot and understood the jealousy which rankled in the heart of Llywelyn. Even amidst the joy at Hafodfraith when they arrived home safely, Meredydd was anxious for the future. But soon after their arrival, a shepherd came bearing the news that Llywelyn had been found lying dead at the foot of a precipice. The thick mist which had brought Meredydd and Elwyn together had led the cruel wizard himself astray.

A short time after, Meredydd and Elwyn married, and the whole neighborhood came together to celebrate their union. They went to live in the white farmhouse on the mountain slope, and thither the good priests of the Monastery of the Standard brought all the gifts bestowed upon Meredydd for his victory over the wyvern.

As time went on, Meredydd and Elwyn's happiness increased. Their children were bold and resolute, and loved and deeply respected their parents. So great a deed as the victory over the wyvern sank deep into their hearts, and the descendants of Meredydd and Elwyn kept the memory of that deed alive with a coat of arms depicting a wyvern, an axe, and a shepherd's crook upon an azure field.

A NOTE ON THE SOURCES

The stories in this book are lightly adapted from tales collected or translated by folklorists and writers in the late nineteenth and early twentieth centuries. They represent a sampling of folklore from four ancient Celtic cultures: Ireland, Scotland, Brittany, and Wales. The stories were excerpted and adapted from the following publications, all of which are in the public domain:

Grierson, Elizabeth, *Scottish Fairy Book, The*. Reprint of the J. B. Lippincott Company 1910 Philadelphia edition, Project Gutenberg, 2011.
http://www.gutenberg.org/files/37532/37532-h/37532-h.htm

Henderson, Bernard, and Stephen Jones, *Wonder Tales of Ancient Wales*. Reprint of the Small, Maynard & Company 1922 Boston edition, Internet Archive, 2007.
https://archive.org/details/wondertalesofanc00hendiala

Masson, Elsie, *Folk Tales of Brittany*. Reprint of the Macrae Smith Company 1929 Philadelphia edition, Sacred Texts, 2004. http://sacred-texts.com/neu/celt/ftb/index.htm

Yeats, W. B, ed., *Fairy and Folk Tales of the Irish Peasantry*. Reprint of the Walter Scott Publishing Company 1888 London edition, Project Gutenberg, 2010.
http://www.gutenberg.org/files/33887/33887-h/33887-h.htm

SOURCES

Assipattle and the Mester Stoorworm
Adapted from "Assipattle and the Mester Stoorworm," by Elizabeth Grierson,
published in *The Scottish Fairy Book*

The Basin of Gold and the Diamond Lance
Adapted from "The Basin of Gold and the Diamond Lance," by Elsie Masson,
published in *Folk Tales of Brittany*

The Black Bull of Norroway
Adapted from "The Black Bull of Norroway," by Elizabeth Grierson,
published in *The Scottish Fairy Book*

The Brownie of Fern Glen
Adapted from "The Brownie o' Ferne-Den," by Elizabeth Grierson,
published in *The Scottish Fairy Book*

The Clumsy Beauty and Her Aunts
Adapted from "The Lazy Beauty and her Aunts," by Patrick Kennedy,
published in *Fairy and Folk Tales of the Irish Peasantry*

The Giant's Stairs
Adapted from "The Giant's Stairs," by T. Crofton Croker,
published in *Fairy and Folk Tales of the Irish Peasantry*

The Kildare Pooka
Adapted from "The Kildare Pooka," by Patrick Kennedy,
published in *Fairy and Folk Tales of the Irish Peasantry*

Little White-Thorn and the Talking Bird
Adapted from "Little White-Thorn and the Talking Bird," by Elsie Masson,
published in *Folk Tales of Brittany*

Master and Man
Adapted from "Master and Man," by T. Crofton Croker,
published in *Fairy and Folk Tales of the Irish Peasantry*

Meredydd and the Wyvern
Adapted from "The Wyvern" and "Meredydd," by Bernard Henderson and Stephen Jones,
published in *Wonder Tales of Ancient Wales*

The Red-Etin
Adapted from "The Red-Etin," by Elizabeth Grierson,
published in *The Scottish Fairy Book*

The Seal Catcher and the Selkies
Adapted from "The Seal Catcher and the Merman," by Elizabeth Grierson,
published in *The Scottish Fairy Book*

The Soul Cages
Adapted from "The Soul Cages," by T. Crofton Croker,
published in *Fairy and Folk Tales of the Irish Peasantry*

Teig O'Kane and the Corpse
Adapted from "Teig O'Kane and the Corpse," translated by Douglas Hyde,
published in *Fairy and Folk Tales of the Irish Peasantry*

The Witch of Fife
Adapted from "The Witch of Fife," by Elizabeth Grierson,
published in *The Scottish Fairy Book*

The Witch of Lok Island
Adapted from "The Witch of Lok Island," by Elsie Masson,
published in *Folk Tales of Brittany*